The Scapegrace

JANET TEMPLETON

DOUBLEDAY & COMPANY, INC.

GARDEN CITY, NEW YORK

1982

All the characters in this book
are fictitious, and any resemblance
to actual persons, living or dead,
is purely coincidental.

Library of Congress Cataloging in Publication Data

Templeton, Janet, 1926–
The scapegrace.

I. Title.
PS3558.E78S28   813'.54
AACR2
ISBN 0-385-17630-9
Library of Congress Catalog Card Number 81–43150

First Edition

For Diana Haviland
with felicitations
from Janet Templeton

The Scapegrace

CHAPTER 1

The hired carriage was turning down along fashionable St. James's Square on a sun-scorched mid-May afternoon in London. Its passenger seats were occupied by a middle-aged man and a young girl whose face was drawn with tension.

The surroundings were notably pleasant, consisting of shops and houses, hitching posts for horses at rest, and the Regent's Guards stationed stiffly at the corners. The young female passenger was not aware of the setting after one quick glance, but looked down hesitantly at herself. She wore a cherry-red walking dress with demure leg-o'-mutton sleeves, and a white pelisse over the shoulders, all intended to set off a complexion that was now even whiter than its usual ivory shade and dark hair under a straw hat.

"I hope this rig-out of mine is to the style here," she murmured.

"You look splendid," her uncle boomed in response. "No need to worry."

Portia Galton, upset as she was, couldn't bring herself to point out that modes played a chief part in any London person's judgment of another. That was her understanding of the prevailing attitudes. Her uncle had been brought up to believe that character is destiny and would never have accepted a revision of that aphorism to say that moral fiber had been replaced by outer raiment. Uncle Stanley Galton was notably out of step in these considerations.

At any other time, Portia would have been touched by his concern for her composure. Her late father's one surviving brother was a portly man with sunburnt features. He jiggled around within his tight-fitting waistcoat over a white shirt and dark trousers, plainly uncomfortable in his best clothes.

"London is only another place to live," Uncle Stanley roared consolingly. He could communicate, it seemed, only by using the topmost register of his voice and had never been afflicted by hoarseness.

It seemed typical of him to think that only the outward face of a difficulty was what mattered, nothing more than some discomfort or readjustment. He was a good-hearted man, so she accepted his estimation for the moment.

"London is not Hove," she insisted correctly, certain that it was a drawback as well as being beyond the slightest question.

"You'll get used to it."

"Tell me one good thing about London, Uncle Stanley. Just one."

"Why, there are any number of good things," the countryman said doggedly. "For instance, there's—ahem! the dozens of eligible young men."

"There are many of those on the beach at Worthing."

"They're richer by far in the city," Uncle Stanley pointed out. Before his youthful niece might make some remark about her attitude toward money, he added, "The playacting, too. That's another advantage to being in London. Kemble and the rest of 'em."

"There's considerable dredging at Shoreham these days too, but I won't take the time to see *that!*"

"There's the opera," Uncle Stanley offered, almost in the same tones as if he himself were performing.

"People bray at each other like donkeys and somebody thinks I'm going to sit and watch."

"Well, there are any number of other points," Uncle Stanley insisted. "Just because I can't think of any at the moment, that doesn't mean the city is without 'em."

The good countryman suddenly turned, his face redder than usual. "You can't stay with me in Sussex any longer, and you know the reason why. Your mam made me promise when she was poorly that I'd bring you out here. She said she had neglected your welfare too long, on account of her own particular lonesomeness. So I have to do this, you know."

Portia nodded reluctantly. Uncle Stanley had helped mother and daughter from the moment that Portia's father was carried off by illness. He had let them stay at the farm, where he and his brothers had raised sheep and some hops and good Sussex lumber as well. He was the only survivor of three boys, the oldest having died after battle during the first war in America.

"And if anything goes wrong out here, niece, you'll still be with family."

"But I don't remember any of them," Portia said quietly. "It's been years since I met them and that was back home. They're complete strangers to me now."

"Your mam's brother and his wife and children aren't strangers no matter how long it's been since you met the elders," Uncle Stanley said fiercely, embarrassed by the emotional content of Portia's confession of the true reason for her insecurity. It was painful that she wasn't close to the people upon whom she would be so dependent. As might have been expected, the countryman brushed it away. To his mind, there was no excuse for any mention of feelings. "It'll be all right, it'll be *all right!*"

By way of changing the subject, he was reduced to praising the look of the area which their hired carriage was traversing, an area he knew because of previous trips to the city to raise money. After Duke Street, the vehicle reached Jermyn at last, navigating carefully in this narrow thoroughfare.

Before Number Sixty-eight, the carriage halted. Portia was looking out at the domicile of her London relatives. She felt unreasonably that first impressions would tell her in advance whether or not a Sussex girl might be happy there. At the initial glimpse of the three-story residence, a distraction took place. The trap flew open overhead and their cabbie's face appeared.

"That's three and six."

Uncle Stanley's jaw fell. "What's that you say?"

"No need to yowl at me, guv'nor," the cabbie said, wincing at his male passenger's bellow. "Three shillin's and sixpence is what yer 'as to brass up."

Uncle Stanley did nothing of the sort. Majestically he climbed out of the cab and scowled up at the driver. "You charge me three and six from the coach halt on Craven Street to this place? Why, you must think I'm fresh from the country and never been out of a hay wain. You must be fit for bedlam!"

Portia, looking from her uncle to the house, felt acutely that she didn't want the London relatives greeting her in the wake of some outrage before their residence. As Uncle Stanley's voice rose even further, hers, from long experience, was lowered.

"Pay it, Uncle Stanley, please."

His attention was caught by the device, as ever, but not to any real purpose. "I won't disgorge that sum, not at all! The blighter can go hang!"

By this time the cabbie had descended from his aerie, a powerful man in his forties, with a paucity of teeth and a surplus of whiskers. In black, including a low-crowned hat with a curly brim, he'd have looked menacing even without a glare and one cocked gloved fist.

"You might be able to shout like 'ell, cocky, but you'd better brass up or I'll show you 'oo's fit for bedlam!"

Portia said quickly, "I'll pay this." She reached across the seat for her reticule.

"Oh no, you don't!" Uncle Stanley roared. "I absolutely forbid it."

Portia wouldn't question an order of her uncle's, certainly not while they were in the presence of another. "At least offer him something!"

"This highbinder doesn't deserve a farthing," Stanley Galton protested. But his niece had been obedient till now and was certainly agitated, so a compromise might not be out of line. "I'm agreeable to an offer of two shillings. That's a sight more than the trip is worth."

"Two shillin's, cocky, and you don't get your girl's bags back." The driver gestured to that hideaway in his ancient place of commercial endeavor which held Portia's effects.

Incensed at the blackmail, as he saw it, Uncle Stanley made two fists and prepared to give battle. The cabbie was keeping one of his own fists primed while he extended the first two fingers of his other hand.

At this juncture, the door of Number Sixty-eight suddenly opened. Portia knew with a sinking feeling that somebody from within would surely know at any moment exactly what was taking place.

The driver, no less angered than his erstwhile passenger, drew to one side nevertheless at the interruption. No doubt he knew the unwisdom of angering some modishly dressed person in this part of London.

It was a regal-looking young man who emerged from the house of Portia's London relatives. Taller than any male in Hove, certainly, and with a sharp nose and keen eyes that didn't remind Portia of her late mother's only brother or his wife, so was therefore unlikely to be possessed by any children of theirs. This young man's outer attire would have startled anyone back in Hove, as he wore tasseled Hessian boots and a long-tailed coat of blue superfine, the whole topped by a high-crowned beaver hat. He carried himself like someone in splendid physical condition. Perhaps he was a sporting man of good income, a member of what London *ton* called the Fancy.

This devilishly handsome apparition's eyes slid away from the sight of cabbie and passenger, but lingered on Portia. She felt a stirring within herself that clashed with her worries of the moment. Hastily she ascribed it to keen regrets that her walking dress, pelisse, and straw were so devoid of flash.

Certainly a man with less of a probing look would have been aware of the unsettled state of her feelings. The conclusions he drew as a result must have caused him to turn and approach the two contestants on the walk.

"What have we here?" the newcomer said in a deep but pleasant voice. "What seems to be the trouble?"

This simple query brought forth a torrent of complaint, each man speaking at once. The cabbie's voice was loud, but Stanley Galton, with wide experience in making himself crystal clear, prevailed again.

"Three and six for the fare from Craven Street is a bam, simply a bam!" he insisted near the top of his lungs.

"So I should think," the young man agreed mildly, instantly adopting Portia's long-time mode for dealing with him. "We can call for a Bow Street beagle to make an end of the matter."

The cabbie winced, well aware that he would lose in such a dispute. Any Bow Street patrol walker would want to play up to that disputant who seemed wealthier.

"It's a matter of simple justice, that's all," Uncle Stanley insisted, mildly for him. "Plain right and wrong are what's at stake here."

The cabbie still looked prepared to mix it up with Stanley Galton and employ bloody violence. Nor would he have shied from fisticuffs with the young man even though it was against his best interests, so inflamed was he.

"*That* would be inadvisable," the newcomer said pointedly, looking down at the cabbie's clenched fists. "Nothing would be settled and all of us would be in a wax at the end of it. One of us is likely to be ill, as a result."

"You're of the Fancy, I takes it, so you think you know what fightin' is," the cabbie sneered. "*I'll* show you what fightin' *really* is!"

"I can spare no time for dramatics," the young man said in languid tones. Portia suspected, however, that the tips of his fingers, now in motion, were beginning to itch. "I have a solution to propose."

"Gimme what I earned, then."

"By the word 'solution' I meant a compromise."

"If I leave without my lolly, the girl in there don't get 'er bag."

"A compromise connotes that all sides will give some leeway." The intruder turned to Uncle Stanley. "How much are you agreeable to offer?"

"Two shillings. It's not worth more."

"Perhaps it deserves another tuppence, but I'm not sure. Very well, then. Give me the two shillings."

Uncle Stanley added a pair of coppers as well, a gesture which the cabbie observed.

"An' now what, guv'nor?" he asked the intruder quietly, somewhat mollified.

"You will deposit the lady's effects on the walk. Then I'll hire your cab and pay the two shillings and tuppence with the fare at my destination."

The cabbie accepted with a nod, not trusting himself to speak his resentment and lose a reasonable compensation.

Portia was aware of the young man opening the carriage door. Briefly she had the notion that he was going to scandalously climb in next to her, but then she saw his extended gloved hands.

"Might I be of assistance, Miss?" he asked softly.

She nodded and put her palm on the back of his hand. The touch was galvanizing and she rose out of the vehicle. Their eyes met and she saw that his were a deep brown, the irises almost as dark as the pupils. She descended and, half a head shorter than he, smiled up, conveying her enormous gratitude to him for having averted possible carnage.

"Your servant," he said.

"Sir, you may assure yourself of my deepest thanks," she responded to his courtesies. Never in life had she spoken with greater sincerity.

He showed pleasure by smiling more widely. Rather than pursue the discussion of his various merits, however, he climbed with grace into the cab. Portia remained too disturbed after the recent upheavals to regret one stranger's imminent departure for the moment, much as she was in his debt.

As the driver was mounting his perch, the new passenger looked away from Portia and addressed him.

"I have no more time to spend away from my destination," he said, making it clear that his hurry to be gone had been inspired from without. "Take me to the Palace Yard, close to the Lords."

Stanley Galton, hearing this request, wouldn't have been surprised at being told that a young man with so much talent for averting struggle in others might be connected with the ruling body of England. The distrait Portia knew she was being stared at until the cab moved, and happened to turn toward her uncle in such a way as to have one last glance at the cumbersome vehicle turning in on the next thoroughfare. The glance had, of course, not been intended.

"I forgot to ask his name," Uncle Stanley boomed, breaking into her thoughts as he would have done by merely taking a deep breath. To Portia's intense surprise he was now smiling down at her. "Niece, I think you've just impressed a sampling of London's wares. I would wager my best snuffbox that you will get used to the city and all its ways. By jingo, yes!"

CHAPTER 2

It seemed to Portia that the difficulties lurking immediately ahead could be no greater than those which had already been surmounted. In this spirit, she accepted her uncle's refusal to accompany her even briefly into the lair of Sir Marcus Kimball and family. He didn't feel comfortable in such flossy dens, as he put it. Portia could understand that. If Stanley Galton said so much as a how-de-do, his voice would probably rattle the sturdy ceilings.

This being so, it became necessary to speak their good-byes on the walk, with Portia's wine-dark portmanteau and varicolored hatboxes nearby. He gave her a discreet kiss, and she knew the good countryman better than to buss and embrace him heartily, as she longed to do.

"We'll write to each other, niece, and I'll make it my business to see you on occasion," he assured her. "So everything will be all right."

"Yes," she agreed lifelessly.

"There's naught for you to worry about," he insisted.

She offered a smile that reassured him because she could call it up from the depths of uncertainty. Uncle Stanley, much relieved, would probably hurry away to one of the boxing saloons and be in a coach for Hove by early nightfall, his sad duty leavened by a dollop of pleasure.

The house, to which Portia now turned, was set farther back from the walk than she had at first realized. It was a good-sized domicile that boasted square curtained windows and a molded front door nobly decorated with a bright polished knocker in the shape of a wreath.

The door was opened wide by a deferential graying man in dark immaculate clothing.

"You're Miss Portia Galton? Welcome, Miss Portia. I am Daltrey."

She had never before seen a butler, let alone spoken to one. Her first impulse was to embrace him in friendship, but his manner made a nod more suitable. She followed that, however, with a far-too-exuberant verbal greeting. Daltrey looked pained, but was at any rate blissfully unaware of the recent *Sturm und Drang* in front of this august residence, and for so much she could be grateful.

As she stepped inside, he was gesturing two liveried footmen to retrieve her impedimenta from the outer precincts. Before he could then direct her any further, Portia was examining the long and narrow anteroom with its highly polished floor in which she could have discerned her reflection. The wooden furniture gleamed as well, angular chairs with a perfectly square table between them on one side. The painting of a hunt scene between two busts on different-sized teakwood pedestals graced the other.

By this time the butler, despite his age, had managed to walk ahead of her and through this anteroom to a double door, which opened at his surprisingly brisk knock. Daltrey stepped nimbly to one side, permitting Portia a view of the arena before she made her entrance.

The drawing-room walls were papered in vertical green and orange stripes, a *motif* carried to the lush curtains in orange and down to the deep carpeting. For the rest, it contained soft chairs and small tables in quantity. It was a room where everything had been calculated to a nicety and nothing was out of place.

A gilt-and-brocade chair at the southwest end was further decorated by the presence of a human form. Dressed in lilac muslin with gigot sleeves puffed out at the arms, her graying hair piled up and to the sides of her forehead, this older woman was Portia's Aunt Beatrice. It took moments to recall her, for each had been styled very differently at their only previous meeting so many years before. Portia would have rushed forward affectionately, but her aunt showed no sign of rising. For the third time in a very few minutes, Portia's natural wish to embrace someone in affection had been soundly thwarted.

"How good of you to come," Aunt Beatrice said, as if Portia had made the choice. It would have been a kind speech, but the flat tone betrayed that she could guess Portia's feelings and was herself accepting a family obligation at her husband's request. She was a woman who could, if she chose, speak volumes in a few words.

"It is good to be here," Portia responded. Surely one untruth deserved another.

Not till then did Lady Kimball gesture Portia to come closer, which the niece accordingly did. Lady Kimball presented a smooth cheek to be kissed, and Portia felt that the exact degree of enthusiasm was mentally noted. The woman apparently wanted to determine how much generosity was being offered before she would give any part of herself. If she gave it all, it would only be in return.

It was a characteristic that was certain to irritate Portia, and she made a point of sitting in a chair that was one removed from that in which she might have been expected to alight. At this, Lady Kimball's pale gray eyes opened wider.

"You will want to refresh yourself after the long journey, I feel sure." It was a dismissal earned by Portia's having put the added distance between them without approval.

"Very soon, of course." The temptation to upset Lady Kimball's most minor calculations was impossible to resist. "But I would hope to first greet my uncle and thank him for his great kindness in allowing me to live here."

"You will certainly be seeing him at supper," Lady Kimball responded.

"Perhaps, then, I could meet both my cousins before doing anything else."

"Your cousin Lionel, I fear, will be away from home for two more days." She shrugged. "As for the sight of your other cousin, of Dulcie, yes, I think you should meet her at this moment. She can deal with the servants while you settle in."

No doubt the opportunity to facilitate matters explained her acceding to a request that she must have known was motivated by little more than willfulness. She rang the handbell, and bade Daltrey ask Miss Dulcie to join her in the lower sitting room.

During the pause, Portia became aware of the older woman looking down and away from her clothes. Lady Beatrice obviously didn't care for the best rig-out that Hove could offer, and forebore to say so at such an early time in their acquaintance. Portia, responding by tactful silence of her own, made no remark about the advantage of the pelisse's clinging so well, or the gown that showed only a nip of the ankle. Her clothes were discreet by necessity and daring by preference, but she kept the peace imposed by the worldly-wise older woman.

There was a distraction before long. A girl entered quickly. She was perhaps a twelve-month younger than Portia, which put her age at nineteen. A blonde in russet, she was adorned in a closed-front gown which fell beautifully and was different from any that Portia had ever seen in Hove. It was the cut that made so considerable a difference, shaping that youthful body to its maximum of attractiveness. Some of her hair was set in cunning half circles across the forehead, and most of the balance was drawn into a knot at the back. The effect recalled a fashion of years ago, but accomplished this minor feat without causing any witness to feel that she was out of style.

It seemed to Portia that the girl was fully prepared to welcome her by a sisterly embrace, but she suddenly paused. Her lips thinned in a wide smile as Portia watched, and a well-tended palm came up to cover them inadequately. She was shaking in mirth, eyes widened unbelievingly on Portia's clothes, on the best that Hove had to offer.

Portia preferred not to become angry as the girl, in this instance like her mother, had not deliberately attempted to be provoking. But some protest was needed, if only to keep her own *amour propre* under this unwitting attack.

"My rig may not fall in with your London ideas, but it is respectable and should not be laughed at."

With an attempt at self-control that seemed little short of miraculous, the blonde composed herself. In doing so, she took note of Portia's features, which were intended to be forbidding but were primarily dismayed. She suddenly became contrite.

"I'm terribly sorry; I truly didn't mean to hurt your feelings."

It was time for Portia to extend the olive branch of forgiveness. "I will probably agree with your tastes very soon, coz, after I've seen the London styles for myself."

"As to that, I can't say." She was aware of Portia deflecting her own anger and added, " 'Coz' indeed! Such is what you call a stranger, while we are to be sisters."

A heart of stone would have been touched by Dulcie Kimball's warmth, and Portia embraced her with a pleasure that was fully returned. It was more than comforting to know that she had taken immediately to an important member of the household.

Politeness now called for Portia to excuse herself to Lady Kimball. The older woman nodded her consent in a suddenly distracted way, then ordered her daughter to be of aid to the newcomer.

Dulcie's response was a clear indication that the wildest of horses would not have kept her from being of service. Chattering away at nineteen to the dozen, she led the delighted Portia out of the room and toward the staircase to the upper recesses of the house.

Lady Kimball, left alone, pursed her lips in thought. She was not best pleased by the character of her husband's late sister's child. She could have put up with the little mischief of undoing orders of precedence upon which the older woman had determined. Indeed Lady Kimball would have relished roundabout disputation on such points. Her children had long accustomed themselves to Mamma's discreet demands, and there was no joy of battle in dealing with them. As for Sir Marcus, her husband always gave a dossier of his day's activities in advance and added the time at which he would return. No, a series of genteel bouts to accustom this stranger to new and more disciplined ways would in themselves have been a source of salt and savor to an older woman.

Far more serious was the difficulty which Portia Galton presented to an ambitious aunt whose life was currently centered on the need to establish her children in the ways that best suited her. Miss Galton was endowed with some wit, as the business of those chairs amply proved. She had the courage to begin a dispute with Dulcie when that child of her aunt's followed the first impulse of laughing at the outlandish clothes, and the diplomacy to be truly forgiving when a sincere apology was tendered. This girl, this Portia, was not bereft of spirit, courage, or mother wit. Compared to the newcomer, her Dulcie was reduced to the status of an agreeable and immature person who was a weathervane for the feelings of others. Lady Kimball was not at all aware what strong influences could have combined to push the spirit and will out of her daughter.

More to the point, however, was that she could foresee fresh problems in the quest for a good position to benefit Dulcie in the marriage market. Her daughter's opportunities could be compromised by the presence of the intelligent and high-spirited Portia in the same family group. Had *she* been a young man, much as it pained her to think so, Lady Kimball knew which of the girls *she* would choose!

It was a challenge that would require some of the shrewdest manipulation of which Lady Kimball was capable. She decided to begin by having a talk with her husband.

Portia had been led up the carpeted steps to that room which had been picked out for her. It was papered in yellow, with white curtains looped at the bottoms, a small table and wooden chair, a soft chair with a brocade pillow and claw legs, and a bureau that might have been made of Sussex oak before being stained a shiny brown.

As soon as her clothing had been put away by servants whose well-trained features betrayed neither censure nor praise, a bath was suggested. In dark muslin robe and satin slippers to match, Portia sallied forth behind Dulcie down the uncarpeted back stairs to a small room in the rear of the house. Here, in a copper-lined fixture of dark wood that looked so sturdy it must also have been grown in Sussex, she sank gratefully into the accepted mixture of six gallons of hot water cooled by two gallons of milk.

Dulcie had hardly stopped speaking, her discourse embracing life in London, of which she decidedly approved. Having mentioned such pleasures of the high season as the Children's Ball, the Concert at St. James's Palace, and the annual Jockey Club Dinner, Dulcie gave a few brief sympathetic words to the current status of Mrs. Fitzherbert, who was the Regent's publicly discarded wife. From there it was a brief transition to talk of the male sex in general and her favorite swains of the moment in particular. These were numerous and attentive, but not, as it happened, sufficiently well positioned to be suitable from Mamma's point of view. Portia kept herself by main force from pointing out that it wasn't Lady Kimball who would be marrying one of these lads, let alone making a life with him.

"I saw a young man leaving this house just before I came in," Portia said, feeling sufficiently at ease in the bath to forget her fevered emotions at the time on account of Uncle Stanley's dispute with the cabbie. "Tall, very handsome, a sharp nose." She decided against adding that she had observed the young man's keen dark brown eyes as well. It wasn't clear whether he was a special favorite of Dulcie's, and not even a detached interest could be shown in him if such was indeed the case.

"That would be Jeremy," Dulcie said with a light laugh, the meaning of which was eventually certain to be clarified.

"He's not your brother, whose name, I am certain, is Lionel."

"No, of course he's not." Another light laugh. "Jeremy came to visit Lionel, but forgot that my brother is far off."

"He isn't a relative at all, then." If the young man had been a family connection, Portia's behavior to him would have been considered rudeness itself, which had been far from her intention.

"Certainly not." She shrugged. "But in another way of speaking, Jeremy might as well be a second brother."

"What do you mean?"

"Why, I've known him since childhood, long before he inherited the title or his seat in the Lords."

"Oh, I see."

"Why, I've known him long before he started riding two-in-hand carriages along the public ways at great speed *pour le sport.*"

Portia supposed that such febrile activity offered a certain relief from the dullness of the Lords, which was fabled through the length and breadth of civilization. It made the young man, who seemed so coolly self-assured suddenly become more human.

"Can you imagine what my life would turn into if he offered for me?" Dulcie asked, simulating a yawn to show that married life with someone she knew so well would hold not the slightest interest for her.

"I suppose, then, that he must feel as you do and will not offer."

"Mamma is most determined, however."

"Do you mean that in spite of your preferences being so clear, your Mamma wants him to offer for you?"

"Him, or somebody of comparable stature. Jeremy, Lord Newlake, has to be considered a catch." Now that the conversation had strayed from areas that excited her, Dulcie settled herself placidly on one of the chairs in this steamy room. "But he isn't a catch to me."

Portia remembered the young man's smile, the brown eyes, the justified self-assurance.

"I don't know him, of course, but I suppose someone without your particular reasons to abhor the prospect could fare considerably worse."

Dulcie, distracted by that tone from further discussion of her own feelings, let out a whoop of unladylike laughter. "Exactly! I have it! What you must do is set your cap for Jeremy."

"But I have no idea whether I like him or not," Portia protested.

"It would be a considerable relief to me if Jeremy were to fall madly in love with you," Dulcie admitted frankly. "I would not always be pestered about him by Mamma and I would be able to cast my net, so to speak, into more interesting waters as far as I am concerned. You surely understand."

"You want me to make myself pleasant (within limits, I presume) to Lord Newlake." Portia mulled it over. "I'll be glad to speak with him again, of course, but I can make no guarantees as to his reaction. He might be immune to my charms."

"Not entirely," Dulcie said with a frank and respectful look that caused Portia to lower her body further into the milk-tinged water. She became aware of her impertinence at that gesture of Portia's and added swiftly, "Your figure in a dress is decidedly comely."

Portia accepted the emendation with a nod, then smiled at the notion of upsetting Lady Kimball even slightly by setting her cap for the first man she had met in London, that man who the knight's wife hoped to sequester for her daughter in spite of Dulcie's finding him unadventuresome.

"Besides, Jeremy is quite decent," Dulcie put in. "He doesn't go in too heavily for the roly-poly or other gambling, and doesn't eat himself into a stupor as many other gentlemen do. You'll like Jeremy, truly!"

"Bless you, sister," Portia said, conferring the honorary title because she was moved by her cousin's genuine warmth and good wishes.

"And may heaven reward your efforts," Dulcie beamed in return, "dear sister."

CHAPTER 3

Sir Marcus Kimball returned to his domain early from an afternoon at Watier's club that had been spiced later on by a view of the racing. Although the exertion of horses did not by itself stir him, the collective felicities had caused him once more to remind himself that he was a deucedly fortunate man. His income was founded on the fact that he was the sole surviving relative, the brother as it happened, of a famous man. Alisdair Kimball (and no one knew for which Scot he had been named) had purchased an Army commission and died bravely at the head of his regiment in a battle with the Americans during that recent disturbance in the former colonies.

Colonel Kimball's heroism had moved many, not least the brother who had always considered him a fool for uniforms and with no more courage than a dollop of chutney. A grateful King in the person of his Regent had knighted the great man's brother and given him a pension that permitted the dazed but grateful Sir Marcus to live comfortably in that mode to which his wife had always hoped to become accustomed. Surely it was an ill wind that blew no one any good. The late Alisdair's *contretemps* on the other side of civilization had been the making of a worthy brother.

He was feeling no surfeit of contentment upon arrival in Jermyn Street, perhaps ten minutes before schedule. A gray-haired man with facial skin that almost matched it, Sir Marcus had managed to remain slim despite his memberships

at Watier's and White's, as well as an occasional evening at
Almack's and frequent dinners with family friends.

Having divested himself of the cloak, which offer was
promptly accepted by the deferential Daltrey, he could be
seen as outfitted in a velvet waistcoat adorned by black-and-
green circles, dark trousers with gold buckles, and boots that
he chose for sturdiness rather than because they were all the
crack; occasionally, and despite his largely abstemious mode
of living, his feet bothered him, and he protected them at risk
to the figure he cut. On the whole, and with various excep-
tions too numerous to be set down, Sir Marcus was a sensible
man.

He wandered into the lower drawing room. By the time as
shown on the thick gold repeater watch whose chain crossed
his slim waist, it was almost the moment he had told his wife
he would be returning.

It struck him promptly that Beatrice was disturbed. After
twenty-one years of connubial bliss interspersed with savage
arguments which he nearly always lost, Sir Marcus could de-
tect her moods more quickly than anyone else.

Lady Kimball had already given some thought to the discussion that was to follow. Her instinct, these days, involved
causing her spouse as little distress as might be possible in
getting her way.

She had become fond of Sir Marcus over twenty-one years.
Marriage to him had been forced on the young Beatrice Armadale by a scheming mother, but instead of regretting it at
leisure, she had come to applaud the choice. From the first,
Marcus had been able to make her respond to stirrings of the
senses, and his skills in that direction caused her to begin
searching more quickly than otherwise for good points about
him in everyday life.

These she discovered shortly. Marcus was thoughtful and
considerate, and didn't often mount a figurative high horse to
declaim that every action involving them must be carried on

in accord with his wishes. It was fortunate, or she would have needed to be even more devious in order to get most of what she wanted in their relations and through their lives together.

"Is everything well?" he began hastily, searching in his mind for sources of possible domestic friction. "I hope that Lionel hasn't written of plans to put a distance from the hearth for a period beyond our expectations."

"No, not at all." Their son was to return from a country visit in a day and a quarter, as she knew precisely. Lady Kimball lowered her voice. "Your niece has arrived."

Sir Marcus had forgotten about Portia Galton, whom he hadn't seen since her childhood. An experienced married man, as has been shown, he could already deduce the probable source of difficulty.

"Hm," he said, rather than make a point of the issue. "What do you think of her?"

"She's a spirited girl, like your late sister was."

"Oh," said Sir Marcus, attempting a fresh sound. His wife possibly felt small relish for lively discussions between aunt and niece which were certain to follow.

"Not that I object to spirit in a girl," Lady Kimball said with some truth, as she had an instinct for taming the unruly. "Such a one will probably catch a man of the rank and position in society that she chooses."

"A pretty girl?"

"Of course she is, if another female sees such prospects as likely. She's also intelligent."

"We won't have her with us for long, in that case." He thought it best to explore the bright side, if she was truly so upset by his niece's presence.

Such optimism deserved to be quenched, in Lady Kimball's view, and the truth of her fears be expressed as a result. "Our Dulcie in turn, as I need hardly point out, is also pretty; but she seems subservient in dealings with young men at her social level and above. Too much of that from Dulcie is certain to make a dismal impression upon a member of the *ton,* by comparison to the other, who is going to be nearby. It is the possible comparison I dread, Marcus—and so should you."

"Perhaps our Dulcie will learn better from my niece."

"Perhaps," Lady Kimball pretended to agree, tight-lipped. Portentously she added, "I have been instructed as to what must be done for the sake of my husband's family obligation to his late sister, and my husband's word has ever been law to me."

That deity accepted the latter statement without demur, proving the effectiveness of Lady Kimball's maneuverings in various directions over the years. He was a man of some sense and goodwill in daily affairs, as has been said, but not a man of keen intelligence in his dealings with others.

"No matter how much more difficult it could make conditions for our dearest Dulcie," his wife concluded, a thoughtful eye on her husband while she dabbed a cambric handkerchief under the lids, "I have to accept the position."

"My dear, I cannot believe that the situation is quite as grim as you indicate," Sir Marcus said. His instinct for the bright side, honed by the happy course his own life had taken as a result of many accidental happenings, had come to the surface yet again. "However, I do say this. I shall be speaking with the girl over supper, and at that time I can judge whether there is right on your side, my dear. If so, I will soon decide what compromises might be adopted as a result."

Despite this *caveat,* Lady Kimball was well satisfied. Sir Marcus might not immediately agree about the need for banishing Miss Galton to those wilds from whence she had erupted, but a beginning had been made and in time his opinion would echo hers. She felt confident of that much.

Portia, blissfully unaware of the plotting against her, dressed eagerly for the supper meeting with her uncle. Upon

Dulcie's approval, she had donned her royal blue silk, which was rated her most suitable supper garment after a long scan of Portia's wardrobe. Forget-me-not flowers were available for Portia's dark hair, and she inserted these herself rather than enlist the services of Dulcie or a maid. She was used to this chore, and it gave time to alter the positioning experimentally. Her instinct had always been to place the three forget-me-nots close to the forehead so that they would be instantly discerned by even the most obtuse spectator. Time and experience had caused a change, and now the decorations were likely to repose almost anywhere else in her dark crown.

As for Dulcie, she was nobly turned out. Her wide-skirted, closed-front gown lay beautifully upon a figure that was now pleasant and which the passing of time would make voluptuous. The pale yellow coloring was superb for her blond hair and light complexion.

Portia met her uncle in the downstairs drawing room and found him a pleasant-spoken man of surprising thinness, in complete contrast to Stanley Galton. Uncle Marcus seemed pleased by her appearance, perhaps only because she was fresh to him and young. Portia relaxed after his first remark about the pleasures of having another daughter under his roof, which she didn't assay as a mechanical courtesy. She felt certain that he would have her best interests at heart.

The dining room was lighted pleasantly by fat wax candles in glass containers. She had taken her place at the huge oval table before realizing that the north wall was a mirror, and presumably one could look in that direction and observe oneself dining. It was a corrective to vanity that would have gained approval from many an ancient philosopher, and Portia couldn't help making an amused comment. Lady Kimball, who had not previously considered that aspect of the matter, responded with an amiability which masked coolness. Portia was aware of her aunt's feelings, and supposed that the older woman was controlling these in her husband's presence.

Lady Kimball spoke hardly at all to Portia over the clear broth with which the meal began. She was forced to apologize to all for the next course, as the haddock appeared to have been both scorched and scalded. Portia offered no comment, as the others did, feeling that it would be an insult added to injury from her aunt's point of view. Lady Kimball, rustling her azure slit sack dress, was quietly angry at what she considered an absence of *politesse*.

"Mistakes do happen," she finally said, eyes glittering. "Dulcie took the wrong attitude to dear Portia's traveling gown, and Portia was quite incensed."

Dulcie said hurriedly, placating her mother, "It was a brief misunderstanding, and I feel sure that Portia and I are good friends."

Portia hastened to agree most sincerely.

Sir Marcus, who truly had no favorable opinion or otherwise about Portia's character, quirked his brows dubiously. "Were you angry at Dulcie, my dear Portia? Dulcie of all people?"

Portia, who had entirely forgotten the incident, looked surprised. "Yes, but it's all over, 'pon my word!"

Lady Kimball riposted demurely, "How good of you to be so friendly to my Dulcie now."

Dulcie, who caught the meaning of that inflection because of long experience with Mamma, bit her lower lip but prudently remained silent. Sir Marcus, his mind not registering that Beatrice had indirectly called his niece a hellion, felt that he reached a guilty verdict by his own reasoning processes. Portia had savagely quarreled with his daughter, the matter soon glossed over—no doubt because of Beatrice's skilled mediation.

Mildly he said, "An equable disposition is important in attracting the interest of some male with whom a girl can make a good marriage."

"My disposition is splendid." Portia smiled at her uncle,

who she still assumed was entirely friendly. "I didn't attack except with words."

Only Dulcie laughed. Sir Marcus looked frozen. Lady Kimball, hearing that Portia had played into her hands, nodded encouragingly.

It was her aunt's behavior which showed that Portia had committed some *faux pas,* and she had no reason to consider the speech any more than a social error of small proportions. She would have offered an apology for ruffling the elders' sensibilities but felt that the matter would by itself soon be forgotten. It could be of no real importance.

The next course arrived at this point. Like all the others it was brought to each diner by a footman and maid under the sharp eyes of old Daltrey standing rigidly behind Lady Kimball's chair during service. It consisted of venison, and boiled potatoes were offered shortly afterward. The knight indulged sparingly, unlike Stanley Galton, thereby showing a gargantuan capacity for self-denial which impressed his niece.

By the time Portia had frankly pronounced the new offering excellent, for she was never sparing of praise, the small upset of a while ago was, to her, a thing of the past.

Not, however, to the knight. Sir Marcus had considered the events of his talk with Portia and was saddened by what he had heard. Even after a few minutes' acquaintance it seemed clear that the girl was blessed with a combination of wit and energy to make Dulcie look, by comparison, pallid in the eyes of any potential suitor. There was some reason, then, for Beatrice's feelings that the proximity of this outlander would hurt Dulcie's opportunities with any male who might otherwise offer for her. At the moment, it was beyond Sir Marcus's ken to evolve a remedy. Nor did he expect much from a female when it came to any discussion of practical matters, but there was always the possibility that Beatrice might later be able to offer a suggestion.

During the service of tea and small square cakes, he caught his wife's eyes and nodded glumly.

It had been planned for the family to attend a musicale at the home of Baron and Baroness Smallwood, but Dulcie insisted that she was poorly. Portia, who would have otherwise joined them, firmly but courteously declined to do anything but stay home and minister to her cousin.

Sir Marcus and his wife did not hesitate to go. Dulcie's upsets were minor and frequent, and Lady Kimball knew with a mother's shrewd judgment that no serious difficulty had arisen. Further, as the Baron was a Scottish peer, it seemed unlikely that the polished ultras of *ton* would appear in force. An invited guest who failed to materialize would not be an object of disapproval. Dulcie gained her mother's permission to avoid the gathering for this reason only.

In the family berline, with two footmen up behind and a sleepy coachman on the box, Sir Marcus and his lady rode down New Burlington Street and cut left to Savile. They were turning right at Clifford Street before Sir Marcus realized that the journey would soon be concluded and that his silent wife was obviously waiting for him to speak on the matter which troubled them both.

"About this problem of my niece," he began diffidently. "I cannot send her back. You surely realize the extent of a family obligation."

"In which case," she returned, looking directly into his eyes, "you have decided what is to be done."

"No, I—I have not reached a final decision as yet," Sir Marcus admitted unhappily.

"We are agreed that there is a problem, but in your eyes the only possible solution is unacceptable."

"I fear so."

"This admits of no alternatives," Lady Kimball pointed out needlessly, "except for likely suitors. Someone like Jeremy

Newlake, for instance, seeing Dulcie with your niece, can be depended upon to be more pleased by a spirited and vigorous girl like Portia."

"That would make a splendid match for her," Sir Marcus said with one of his intermittent attacks of optimism.

"And every member of *ton* would point out that Dulcie remains a spinster while her cousin came up to the city and instantly made a great conquest! The question that would follow on every pair of lips would then be 'What is wrong with Dulcie Kimball?' Can you imagine those words on the lips of Lady Jersey, Lady Cowper, or the other patronesses of Almack's? Parents of marriageable sons would be incited to discourage any hope of connubial bliss for Dulcie. And all because of this newcomer, this niece of yours."

It was on the tip of Sir Marcus's tongue to say that Beatrice was putting it rather strongly, but he didn't feel entirely certain of that much.

"Do you have a suggestion I can accept?"

Lady Kimball shifted her body slightly in the lap robe which she utilized when in the family carriage whatever the season.

"An idea just occurred to me because of what you said," Lady Kimball smiled with notable disregard of truth. She was referring to a notion that had stirred in her mind during what she considered Portia's graceless behavior at supper. "I shall put it plainly. Miss Galton has come to the city to make a marriage, and I now think it should be accomplished quickly as possible."

"But you were just saying—"

"My thought is that she wed, but not to one of the *haut ton*. If she weds in a lower class it would dispose of comparisons and the threat she is to the prospects of our ninnyhammer of a daughter."

Sir Marcus considered. No other possibility would permit

his living up to the letter of that sacred obligation to his dear sister's memory.

"A military man, perhaps," he suggested. "One could hardly find a more upright and respectable class that is not of the polished exclusives. My late brother, for example, founded our fortunes indirectly by giving his life for the King while in the Army."

"I shall dredge up an Army man for her."

"No, I'll do that myself. I wish to be certain that Portia is wed to a decent and honorable man of good prospects. To facilitate matters with a man who may not be affluent, I plan to provide a splendid dowry."

And Sir Marcus gave a firm nod, having reached this decision with the aid of his dearest Beatrice. He was well satisfied.

CHAPTER 4

Sir Marcus felt less interest in the sport of kings than in the need to show himself where some of the *ton* would be gathered. As a result, he found himself next afternoon across the river and a restless spectator at the Egham races.

Lacking an interest in the fortunes of various horses designated as Arab, Turk, or Barb, and convinced that the place for horses was in a stable or in front of a moving carriage, Sir Marcus looked around him at the other spectators. Young dandies and older ones, dissipated rakes and gout-infested clubmen could be seen in almost any direction. Sir Marcus exchanged *mots* with "Comical Bob" Spencer, youngest son of the Duke of Marlborough. He found himself cheek by jowl with the Right Honorable Septimus Avery, an impecunious offspring of the peerage who was troubled by gout in a thumb, as he explained without being asked. The pain had traveled from the littlest finger on his right hand to the thumb of his left, and two doctors had already bled him to no effect. The Right Hon. was, he put it sadly, a picture of ill health. So preoccupied with his own condition was he that one could expect him to recite the names of various fevers assailing his body at the same time. These colorful indispositions never caused him to miss a race meeting or a rout, however, let alone a ball; and he was a favorite of the *doyenne* of demireps herself, Miss Harriette Wilson.

Sir Marcus, bearing in mind the mission with which he had entrusted himself, looked around for someone else who might offer guidance in the matter of finding an impecunious military man who could aspire to some of Sir Marcus's money allied with Portia's hand in marriage. He rejected half a dozen fops and reprobates as sources of information during a between-races walk, and nearly stumbled across Jeremy, Lord Newlake.

Jeremy happened to be bearing sou'west when the mishap occurred. Later, Sir Marcus would inform his dear wife waggishly that he had fallen over Jeremy's sharp beak, but at the moment of impact he was discomposed and out of breath.

"My dear boy," he said when he had recovered, indicating with a palm that no major damage had been done. Jeremy was a prospective son-in-law and certainly entitled to every courtesy until the wedding day. "I hope I haven't upset *you*."

"Not at all, Sir Marcus," Jeremy said, so offhandedly that something else was plainly occupying his thoughts. "Quite the contrary. I had hoped you would be among those present in this great throng. You are the one man in London or its environs that I most want to see."

"Well, I'm flattered, certainly," Sir Marcus returned, managing to exude *bonhomie* without the least trace of obsequiousness. He could understand Jeremy's interest in attending this equine gala, as Jeremy liked to sport-race a carriage along the narrow London streets, taking care to harm as few pedestrians as possible. He hoped for his daughter's sake that Dulcie would not be afflicted with the need to attend race meetings if Jeremy chose her in the marriage market. "But I can assure you I have no inside information as to the capacities of these animals. None in the world."

"That is hardly necessary," Jeremy smiled. "I will inform you, parenthetically, that if you wager on Martinique in the next race your money will be returned tenfold, like bread upon the waters. Martinique runs while the other horses will, by comparison, be strolling in a dignified manner."

"Thank you." Sir Marcus had other uses for the needful than gambling it away where none would know of his losses or believe his gains. "Could I ask why it is that my company is so welcome to you at this juncture? I am pleased certainly, as I have indicated, but would have expected you to prefer the company of jockeys and trainers at such a time."

"Permit me to explain." Jeremy shot the cuffs of his tight-fitting black tailcoat, then touched a palm to the discreet Osbaldestone knot of his snowy cravat. "It is a plain matter."

The parliamentarian was hesitant. Sir Marcus, watching with suddenly narrowed eyes, decided that the young peer had finally set himself to ask permission for paying addresses to Dulcie. It was a disconcerting time to bring up the matter, but Sir Marcus was rarely surprised by the thought processes of youth. He was, after all, a father.

Jeremy began to speak his mind. "It's about a girl."

"Yes?"

"A very pretty girl."

Sir Marcus was mentally confounding the young man for his roundabout speaking manner, which went far to explain why a debate in the Lords could stretch from January to December with no decision made. His smile was in place, however, his demeanor unruffled. He was prepared to congratulate the young hound in a moment, and to look properly surprised and pleased as well.

"I don't know exactly how to put it, Sir Marcus, but I would appreciate being told something about the very pretty girl I saw in front of your house yesterday afternoon."

It took a moment for the knight to realize that Jeremy, Lord Newlake, was making this reference to some strange girl who had apparently materialized before Sir Marcus's domicile in the recent past. The notion of himself as a father-in-law soon to be a grandfather, and all the rosy little images that had accordingly crowded into his head, promptly receded as if they had never been.

"I see." He would not lose his temper before this young

whelp. "You expect me to know every passerby along the front of Number Sixty-eight Jermyn Street."

"No, not at all. This one had halted a hired carriage before your home, so I assume that she, with an older man, was going inside." His voice softened. "A dark-haired filly with the greenest eyes a man will ever see, and the pearliest skin."

Sir Marcus kept from asking if Jeremy had counted the creature's teeth. He was not obtuse in dealing with others of his sex, however, and now knew perfectly well that it was his niece to whom Jeremy was referring. This line of questioning must be put to rest.

"I haven't the foggiest," Sir Marcus said, lying with a straight face. "I hardly keep a stable of females in my home, to use an image that you would surely understand. A young one and an older are quite enough for any rational man."

"In that case, we will give no further attention to the matter," Jeremy said, making a mental note to inquire of Dulcie about the ravishing creature's identity. "It can be of no true importance."

"No, certainly it can't." A possible explanation occurred to Sir Marcus, offering enough of unwelcome speculation so that the young man would forget this matter. "My wife may have hired a new maid, and perhaps that is who you saw. I'll be glad to inquire, if you like."

"Don't trouble yourself, Sir Marcus." Jeremy couldn't help experiencing a moment's disappointment, having looked forward to dancing attendance on that lovely female. The explanation as offered could be entirely correct. Certainly the girl had been dressed in clothes that didn't resemble any that had appeared for a long while on a London girl of *ton*. Leg-o'-mutton sleeves, if he remembered aright! In which case, it seemed more than probable that she was of the low orders and held no interest to him, except as a feast for the eyes and the imagination.

Sir Marcus, having received further proof of the need to

marry off his niece with all dispatch, cleared his throat as Jeremy started to disengage himself.

"One moment, please."

"I am, of course, your most obedient servant, but the next race is about to be run and no conversation will be possible."

Indeed there came to the older man's ears a hubbub of noise and cheering that made him wince. Looking out to the field, Sir Marcus saw a number of horses proceeding in a frenzy down the track on this sunny May afternoon, not at all held back by a stone's added weight or so that was intended to equalize their chances. It was like a parody of some military charge. To his jaundiced eye, each of the beasts was indistinguishable from the others. Jeremy, of course, did not experience such a difficulty.

"Run on, Martinique!" he shouted at the top of his lungs. In this moment he was far removed by temperament from the judicious and discreet young man who was admired through the length and breadth of London. No doubt he found relief from the serenity of the day in outbursts of fury. Sir Marcus accepted this manifestation but didn't understand it in the least.

The horse must have agreed with Jeremy's exhortations to greater effort, as every contender was in rapid motion. Martinique, however, must not have been performing satisfactorily.

"Oh, hang it!" Jeremy said in agony, lips drawn thin as that mild expletive was followed by one savage curse after another.

The circular charge had come to an end. Apparently the wondrous Martinique had finished as one of the cluster who trailed another of his zoological *confrères*.

"I should have guessed that no other Arab would win if Escape was in the race," Jeremy groaned when the audience sounds subsided long enough for him to remember that he was in the presence of another. "A late entry, of course, and I was too absorbed in conversation to hear the announcement."

"I beg your pardon for having distracted you, Jeremy."

"Not in the least. Your talk was absorbing, as ever, so that there was an ample reward."

He had recovered his manners, and Sir Marcus courteously responded with a question to pretend some interest in the affair.

"Escape? Is that also the name of a horse?"

"The Regent's best," said Jeremy sadly.

Sir Marcus followed the young man's look out at the royal box, and now his interest was at least briefly piqued. The heir to Britain's throne was rejoicing with others in the victory of his animal. For this occasion the Regent wore a claret-striped silk coat and breeches, and a waistcoat embroidered with silver and stones. Diamonds served his coat for buttons. To Sir Marcus, who dressed with the moderation that Mr. Brummell and others of the Dandy Club favored, the Regent was piebald and fatter than his horse.

Sir Marcus, lowering his quizzing glass, made a sound of muffled disapproval. Jeremy assumed that the reaction was caused by the Regent's thoroughgoing lack of good sportsmanship and smiled companionably. Having thus inadvertently established himself as an ally of Jeremy's, Sir Marcus decided to take instant advantage of the status conferred on him.

"I know, of course, that I can trust your discretion," he began, referring to the difficulty posed by Portia Galton's presence in his home and the need to find a spouse who wasn't quite *ton* or disgrace Dulcie, his daughter, forever. Not knowing who might overhear too much in this semipublic area, he chose to be indirect. "I take it, my dear Jeremy, that you have many acquaintances among military types."

Jeremy didn't seem startled by an apparent change of subject. He had, as a matter of fact, been briefly gazetted to the

Coldstream Guards before his late father shipped him to Oriel College at Oxford, in hopes of gaining him the influence for a career in politics. Jeremy could have pointed out that he remained on speaking terms with at least one sergeant, two corporals, a drummer, and any number of private dragoons. In this peacetime year of '16, that was no small achievement.

"You do not refer to enlisted men?"

"Certainly not."

Jeremy was acquainted with a few officers as well, men who were always cock-a-hoop and walking proudly in their varicolored military dress uniforms topped by wigs that had been crinkled and plastered and powdered. A group of men whose minds were forever closed to compromise, to reason. All except for the Duke of Wellington, for Old Hookey himself, who forever remained the exception to prove any rule.

"Young officers," Sir Marcus added.

"Are there are any other stipulations about these military men you ask of? If so, I will be able to think ahead more clearly if I am told what those might be."

Sir Marcus realized that the young man's patience and diplomacy were exemplary but not infinite. "They must want to advance their careers but be unable to do so because of money."

As Sir Marcus fell silent, Jeremy pondered.

"I feel sure that any number of such men are currently in the King's service," he said, discreetly avoiding those questions that came first to mind.

"One will be sufficient for my purpose if he is indeed promising," Sir Marcus responded. "I don't want to find myself confronting some lackwit who would be content with a dowry above his stipend, and both followed by a pension." He felt righteously that Portia deserved better from the man chosen to marry her. "I care not if his family connections aren't those of a polished ultra. Not every unmarried officer has these to offer."

Sir Marcus was trying to show by those last words that he could be liberal in outlook. He had, instead, succeeded in chilling his listener.

For Jeremy now understood that Sir Marcus and presumably his wife were searching for a young unmarried officer. In return for a good financial settlement, this young man was to wed. Jeremy could not possibly doubt that the intended bride was Dulcie, Sir Marcus's only daughter.

It was logical, too, that an admirer of the military such as Sir Marcus was, and indeed a man whose brother had perished in the service of Bulldom, would seek a military man as Dulcie's husband. Sadly, the elder couple had surrendered any hope of their daughter's marrying well. No doubt Sir Marcus himself would have spoken more to the point, but he surely had no wish to be overheard discussing so sensitive a matter in any public place.

"And you want the name of such an officer from me," Jeremy mused.

"One or more, to be sure."

"I feel certain that for a good cause I can find the best men." Certainly he would make the most diligent efforts to aid Dulcie, who had been a friend since childhood. "And of course he must be handsome and well mannered."

"Neither of those qualities can do the least harm, but they are not of paramount importance, either."

"To reach the best possible candidates I will spur my recollection and make inquiries of friends. I will even repair to Stephen's on Bond Street if necessary." He referred to a hostelry at which many Army men stayed overnight during time that had to be spent in *le monde*. "Indeed I shall begin immediately, being glad to leave this establishment in which the racing regulations are changed at the whim of a ruler"—he gestured around him—"and report to you as soon as may be."

"Tonight?" There was no time to be lost. "I can meet you at Watier's, say, by ten o'clock."

"The food at Watier's is excellent, but eating with friends is preferable. If such is among the possibilities, I should arrive later by far than ten."

Jeremy had planned on dining with some friends of his youth at the home of one of them. Sir Marcus, misinterpreting because his senses were tuned for shades of meaning where they might not exist, felt that he was being pointedly asked to issue an invitation for the young peer to dine at Jermyn Street. A way would be found to keep Portia out of his sight.

"Come to my digs for the six o'clock feeding and when it's done you can let me know of your progress in the matter at hand."

Jeremy felt certain that the impatient Sir Marcus would accept no alternative. As he had already volunteered his services on Dulcie's behalf, he nodded agreeably now.

"I will be honored to join you and your family, Sir Marcus," he smiled. "And I am most grateful to have been asked."

CHAPTER 5

Portia looked forward to a pleasant afternoon in which she
and Dulcie would make visits to family and friends of her city
cousin. Perhaps Lady Kimball would join them, decreasing
the afternoon's pleasantness somewhat for her niece. The
spirited and often impetuous Portia felt little love for that cal-
culating and temperamentally affected woman who was her
aunt.

In preparation for such innocuous diversion, Portia had
dressed in a sprigged muslin with turquoise coloring to show
off the light complexion which was one of her great assets. In
the upstairs drawing room she found Dulcie picking feebly at
a spinet, at which she had become proficient under maternal
duress and with no distinction whatever. At Portia's appearance in the sunny room, she halted.

"Mamma insisted that I acquire this social accomplishment," she said, rising. "I would have preferred the flute,
but Mamma ruled that such an implement (as she called it)
is not suitable for a female."

The two girls embraced.

"Oh, we're going to have a lovely afternoon, I just know it,"
Dulcie gushed, having been first to disengage. "We will get
the vis-à-vis carriage with Passy to drive it and go into Hyde
Park together."

"It seems an aimless excursion."

"Quite the contrary." Dulcie raised a hand to her lips,
muffling a short laugh. "Hyde Park by day is simply a dandy's
cave."

"Dandy? Men, you mean."

"Certainly I do. Dandies and Army men and those from the Navy who might be in London. We drive past and smile, and perhaps, if we wish to, we stop and engage in some *pour-parlers* with them. But only if they are comely."

The schedule did indeed, upon consideration, appear suitable for a gratifying few hours, even though Portia believed that no young man could be more comely than that efficient peer she had met yesterday in front of this house and whose name she later learned was Jeremy Newlake. But if a carriage ride *à deux* was Dulcie's idea of the finest possible amusement, Portia would participate at least once.

"How soon do we leave?"

"In moments, now that I have your approval. I will instruct Daltrey to see that the carriage is made ready."

Just as she approached the wine-dark bellpull by the window, Lady Kimball's voice rang out:

"You will do no such thing."

Portia's aunt had opened the door stealthily and no doubt listened long enough to absorb the sense of what was being said. She stood upright, gray hair parted and pulled back in a knot, body tensely alert for dissension to be quashed on the instant. Her day dress, in orange and with a surprisingly low neckline, was perfectly styled without corresponding good taste, as if Lady Kimball was determined to wear what she felt suitable and even to make it so by her choice.

"Oh, but Mamma!" Dulcie started, shocked by the beldame's refusal to let her and Portia take the vis-à-vis into Hyde Park for an outing among the dandies.

Lady Kimball announced, "There is another matter of even greater importance which must be attended to."

"Some visit?"

"Not to a person as such. To a *modiste* and her shop."

At the prospect of acquiring new clothes, Dulcie's aspect changed until it was noticeably lacking in sullenness.

"I am pleased, of course, Mamma, but I do think that my wardrobe will be sufficient for the day."

"Yours, yes."

Dulcie blinked. "I see now, Mamma, of course. It is Portia whom you wish us to shop for."

"I plan to take Portia with me, but you are at perfect liberty to go with a friend to Hyde Park and tease the gentlemen, if that is what you wish."

"Oh, Mamma, I couldn't be kept away from a shopping expedition. How delightful to be purchasing a new wardrobe, and for Portia."

Smiling, Portia spoke from a full heart. "I am most grateful for the attention, Aunt Beatrice."

"A fresh wardrobe is no more than you need for the city," Lady Kimball answered properly but without corresponding warmth. "Else your uncle and aunt and cousins would be shamed."

Hearing that tone, it sadly occurred to Portia that her perception of suitable clothes wouldn't agree with Lady Kimball's. This particular mission, which ought to have been a delight, would probably pose difficulties.

Dulcie, all unaware of Portia's feelings, asked eagerly, "When do we embark on this voyage of discovery for Portia?"

"Immediately."

The girls left for their respective rooms to don appropriate bonnets and accompany those with parasols. Dulcie was chattering when they joined Lady Kimball before the house. The family berline waited at the curb with a coachman up and two behind.

Lady Kimball, utilizing her lap robe, therefore insisted that the girls follow her example. Dulcie began singing the praise of Madame Yvonne, the *modiste* on Bruton Street. When she called that Frenchwoman the best practitioner of her craft in *le monde*, Lady Kimball judged that it was time to interpose herself.

"I am taking Portia off to Mademoiselle Sylvia on Chandos Street."

"Sylvia?" Dulcie was shocked. "But her goods are tawdry by comparison."

"Not at all."

"Certainly they are cheaper, Mamma. All of London knows that Sylvia's gowns are cheaper in price, because they are not as well executed as Madame Yvonne's."

"Silence!" Lady Kimball ordered.

Dulcie obeyed, biting her lower lip and looking sympathetically in Portia's direction. As for the latter, she turned sharply to stare out the nearest window. She was so upset that she was hardly aware of the bright-colored houses on two sides of her. Not till the carriage made a turn between a pair of hay wains did she become aware of a sign that advertised a *modiste*'s place of business. Chandos Street had been reached at long and silent last.

Sylvia's store front boasted two windows with opulently dressed simulations of the female figure. In the showroom, with candlelight magnified by bowls with oriental-inspired designs, the figures were attired in more easily discernible whites and shades of red. Ball gowns could be seen, with day dresses and a nightgown or two. Here, indeed, was a concatenation of diligently shaped clothes, but without the meticulous crafting of Dulcie's rig-out or Lady Kimball's. The situation was as horrendous as Portia had feared.

She was aware of a commotion nearby, and a beaded curtain opened on a middle-aged woman who rushed forward to greet Lady Kimball.

"Why, what a wonderful surprise," said this apparition, speaking English without any trace of French accent. "I can't hardly believe my eyes, I can't. Lady Kimball, it's an honor to have you in my establishment. How can I be of service to you?"

Mademoiselle Sylvia had apparently not gallicized her

given name because she was so inflexibly British that no one would have credited any claim of foreign origin. The speech and manner, even the cut of her clothes, had a roast-beef-and-kidney-pudding air, as Portia put it to herself. The woman was certainly in her forties, hair brighter than Dulcie's blond locks and fashionably shaped in ringlets over the forehead and the balance pulled back to end in a dainty knot. She wore a largely azure day dress with a detachable bib front, and the tiniest shoes that Portia had ever seen on a full-grown female. Portia liked her but didn't have the least fondness for the clothes displayed across various mannequins on the glossy showroom floor.

"What you can do," Lady Kimball replied slowly, "is to set out a wardrobe for my niece here. She has just emerged from Sussex."

"Your niece?" Sylvia smiled across at her. "But how charmant!"

The French word was spoken with a wholly British inflection. Portia, herself no linguist, couldn't help wincing.

"But we've got just the things, of course! Where shall we start?"

"With the outer covering," Lady Kimball said dryly. "The inner workings, so to speak, will remain out of sight for a while and can be attired when the need arises."

"You mean when a gentleman comes along to make an offer," Sylvia chuckled. "May ooee!"

With this agreement and the help of three twittering workers, the shoppers viewed a number of dresses for all possible occasions and with every conceivable decoration. Some were braided and others embroidered, some adorned with lace knots or ribbons, others with spangles, red rosettes, and similar distractions.

Portia was determined in fairness to judge each dress upon its merits. The certainty that Lady Kimball wanted to dress her in second-best effects kept her silent and withdrawn.

Holding her tongue while examining the ill-cut clothes was almost a physical labor.

Lady Kimball soon grew tired of this sport. She gave an irritable toss of the head and claimed to like the next item set forth in front of her and the young girls. This was a ball dress of dark blue and bordered in gold.

"Lovely for you, my dear," she said to Portia. "Properly modest and enticing. Most suitable."

"Your pardon, Aunt Beatrice, but I don't agree." There was a line of moisture on Portia's forehead, so tense was she.

"Surely you can have no objection to this splendid gown. When it is worn on your figure you will catch the attention of any male whatever, and I feel sure I am not the only one who would say so."

At this juncture she looked to her daughter for support. Dulcie, warned by the speech, had taken good care to turn away so as not to be asked for an opinion already determined by her domineering mother. By this time, she realized what lay behind Mamma's choice of a *modiste* for Portia, and was appalled by such horrid calculation.

Lady Kimball withdrew any attempt to capture her daughter's wandering attention, convinced that Dulcie would offer only the weakest support. Unaided, she charged into the fray.

"Can you give even one reason why this gown is unsuitable?"

"I don't believe it brings out the color of my eyes properly," Portia said. Even now, she chose a politic reason apart from quality, although it needed a pause to make up her mind. In that time Lady Kimball bridled further.

"What nonsense!" she said almost before her niece was finished. She had little feeling for color in the best of circumstances and wanted mostly to leave this refuge for cheapjack finery with her self-appointed task completed. "Your eyes are perfectly adequate, as any suitor will notice in this gown."

"But I want a gown that will help convince some gentleman that my eyes are magnificent," Portia responded.

The *modiste*, with a belated long look at Portia's striking dark green eyes, interrupted before Lady Kimball could resume the attack.

"I can offer almost the same cut in apple green and—"

"This gown is perfectly splendid," Lady Kimball pronounced. "As a young woman I would have been thrilled at wearing this."

"Perhaps," Portia said quickly, "you would have been more suited to it."

"Nonsense!" Lady Kimball briefly considered that her late mother, Mrs. Armadale, would have almost certainly bullied her into the purchase of something else that was perfectly dreadful. Lady Kimball thought of herself as strong-willed, like her mother, but only for other people's best interests. "With white gloves and a gold-dusted reticule, you will be most attractive."

Portia spoke carefully, unused to outright quarrels with her elders but determined not to give in. "I would not be happy in this."

"When you try it on, young lady, we shall all see how suitable it is. Sylvia, prepare a robing room for my niece."

Dulcie, observing Mamma's increasing temper and fearing a full-blown scene, said quietly, "Yes, you ought at least to try it on, Portia dear."

It occurred to Portia that someone as skilled in dealing with others as that handsome Jeremy Newlake would have handled some corresponding difficulty and sowed good feelings in his wake as well. The capacity to speak her mind, yet earn the respect of all, was more than the straightforward girl could muster.

"I can wear this in the shop, but later on I will make excuses not to wear it ever," she said. "I do not like this dress and cannot be happy in it."

Lady Kimball's lips became a thin angry line, then she turned imperiously to the *modiste*. "When my niece comes to her senses, the garment can be altered to fit." She would make her point by direct and continual discussion at home. Exactly as if Portia had approved of the gown, she added, "We will take it."

Dulcie, who hadn't realized that Mamma would ever avoid a confrontation, looked with open-mouthed admiration at this cousin, this girl who had stood up to vested authority.

The *modiste* had probably encountered more horrendous scenes in her shop. Now she said only, "I hope I may serve you and your daughter and niece again."

Lady Kimball left, adopting a stately pace. In the street, she loudly instructed one of the coachmen to retrieve her purchase.

Portia, on her way out of the shop and preceding a still awestruck Dulcie, heard the *modiste* draw a deep breath and speak in the worst possible French.

"Soot al-ors," Mademoiselle Sylvia murmured, trying to sound philosophical and make herself heard as exuding a continental sophistication. "I say, yes, soot al-ors."

CHAPTER 6

The return to Jermyn Street might have been an occasion of mourning, with Lady Kimball grimly silent and Dulcie staring in awe from one former contestant to the other. Portia, ready to take up the cudgels once more if necessary, sat with tightly folded hands while she watched London pass before her.

Arrived at home, Dulcie insisted on joining a bone-weary Portia in the latter's room, sitting on the brocade pillow in her soft chair and repeatedly telling Portia how she felt about the miracle that had happened. Portia turned to the door, making certain that Lady Kimball didn't once again surprise her by a sudden entrance.

Dulcie's thoughts moved to what she considered were practical matters. "Tonight you must tell my father what happened just now."

"I'd like to," Portia admitted, "but I cannot take the chance of possibly making him angry at me too."

"Father would certainly remark about the purchase of a dress you have no plan to wear."

"Gentlemen aren't surprised by heated discussions about clothes among the female sex," Portia said, thinking of her Uncle Stanley.

Dulcie was not to be swayed. "Father would then ask what's wrong and why you can't have a gown you like. Mother would hesitate and I would confirm the truth quickly, so that Mamma couldn't deny it. That will be too delicious, Portia, and you must do it."

Having seen her mother discomfited on one occasion, Dulcie wanted another experience of that type.

"No, I can't be party to any conspiracy. Such maneuvering goes against me."

"But how can any female gain what she wants if she doesn't use bounce?"

It was a speculation that could have caused an argument for days, but Portia cleared her throat as the door silently opened.

With exact truth and no welcome whatever she said, "Aunt Beatrice, you are here."

Lady Kimball was not embarrassed at knowing that one of her small but previously serviceable ruses had been discovered and anticipated. In Portia Galton she had found, to be sure, a foe worthy of her steel.

"You have been invited to take supper with the Marquess and Marchioness of Eastwood," she said, referring to an arrangement she had perfected as soon as Sir Marcus told her of having invited Jeremy Newlake to supper in Jermyn Street. "The berline will take you at five forty-five."

"I shall be glad to sup with the Marquess and Marchioness."

Lady Kimball misunderstood the strict courtesy in Portia's words, assuming that the young girl meant it would be preferable to spending part of one night at Lady Kimball's table.

"Unfortunately," she said, stung into reminding Portia of the day's event, "you have nothing to wear for the occasion, as your new gown has not (because of your stubbornness) had the few necessary alterations for a perfect fit. You will, however, have to make the best of it with your country clothes."

Portia wanted to retort that she could afford to purchase the clothes of her choice because of the money that Uncle Stanley had given her. Such actions would have been extremely disrespectful, as she knew, so she said nothing and would have to refrain for a while from any purchases of clothing in line with her own tastes.

Lady Kimball, having made this point and struck back at impertinence, left without another word or a look at her daughter.

Portia exchanged glances with Dulcie. It seemed clear that she was being banished for the night because her aunt was displeased with her.

Dulcie, however, had evolved another explanation. "She's keeping you from seeing Father, because she expects you'll make a complaint about the afternoon's difficulty."

"I could make the same complaint tomorrow night."

"By then she will have concocted some other stratagem to keep you silent." Dulcie spoke with the sadness of great experience.

An explication along those lines hadn't occurred to Portia but seemed quite likely. Because Dulcie was thoroughly cowed by Lady Kimball, the older woman expected her niece to be repressed with one device after another.

Portia accepted this without question. Grim resolve stiffened her spine.

"In that case, I'll wear the infernal gown this evening and for a little while in the house."

"What?"

"I'll put it on at five-thirty and go to the downstairs drawing room, where my uncle takes some refreshment before he sups."

"Usually he does, yes."

"There I will tell him exactly what took place today and show him the result," Portia said determinedly. "If I do it that way, he'll certainly be able to see for himself the bad cut and coloring of the garment. There will be no beating about the bush."

The gown had been brought into the room earlier by Humility, Lady Kimball's maid. Portia conquered her repugnance and put it on, with Dulcie's delighted help. It didn't have the instant yielding quality of better-cut fabrics, but surprisingly little alteration would be needed if she ever intended to actually wear the horror. Only slightly overlong at the hem, she decided, and one of the bombazine sleeves could have been comfortably crimped at the wrist. All in all, however, an uglier garment for her own use couldn't have been conceived. Of that much she felt certain.

"Ghastly," Portia decided, examining herself in the oversized mirror on the north wall.

"In a dim light it would look no worse than unfortunate," Dulcie concluded.

"Rather as if someone had started out to design a suit of chain mail and changed her mind at the last minute."

Portia decided on waiting until a moment before five-thirty to go down, doing it before Lady Kimball might come back to chortle wickedly over whichever female regimentals were picked for supper with a Marquess and Marchioness. She took it for granted that her uncle would be settling in the drawing room. In Sussex, her Uncle Stanley always lurked there for three quarters of an hour before supper, and Portia had been taught that all gentlemen waited avidly to dine. With the interview completed, she could then return upstairs and change for the night's visit.

Having embraced her cousin, Portia started down the stairs. She lifted the gown slightly so that its hem wouldn't touch the gleaming wooden floor in her rush across the hallway. The drawing-room door was wide open and she rushed in, then looked around swiftly.

On a soft chair, a copy of Leigh Hunt's newspaper *The Examiner* on his buckled breeches, elbows tapping against his pinched-in jacket with surprise, sat Jeremy, Lord Newlake.

It would be an exaggeration to say that Portia's jaw dropped noisily, but in truth she was appalled. She had looked forward to seeing him again at a time and place of her own choosing and when dressed to the nines, not while apparently trying to look like a chambermaid in shoddy superfine.

"You can't be here!" she started, speaking the first words that rose to her lips.

"Oh, but I am," Jeremy said in that thrillingly deep voice she remembered so well and that sent little shivers of joy through her. He rose politely and glanced around at the vertical green-and-orange-striped wallpaper. "I quite assure you that I am here."

"But where's my unc—Sir Marcus?"

"I can only assume that he has been delayed." Perhaps he felt that a compliment would better serve to put her at ease. "A decidedly fortunate circumstance, I do believe."

His gallantry was in direct opposition to Portia's own confused thoughts. He was smiling into her face and she became aware that he was inspecting the light complexion under dark hair in half ringlets over the forehead and pulled back, as well as the dark green eyes.

"I had asked after you because of our first accidental meeting in front of this domicile, but received no information of substance. This time I am determined to find out who you are and what good omen has brought you to these precincts."

Portia saw his glance briefly venturing lower and then returning back to meet her eyes. She assumed that his speech and manner were part of his diplomatic instincts and that he couldn't think of her as at all comely or intelligent.

Rather than pretend that she was being admired, Portia sadly started to turn and leave. In her upset she had lost her hold on the nether part of the garment and one of her white satin slippers bit into its hem. The room began to whirl and she knew her balance was gone.

Where another man would have laughed at this *gaucherie*, Jeremy Newlake rushed forward to keep her from falling. She made an impact against him, herself galvanized by the contact.

She looked up promptly at the tall peer, wanting to let him know firmly that she was well. His face was close and he stared into her eyes. That was when his lips came down to hers and she was being soundly kissed. Impossible to doubt any longer that he found her comely! In her astonished happiness, Portia never recollected if she was of assistance by returning the pressure.

There was a slight draft through the wide-open door and, reminded of the surroundings, Jeremy raised his lips from hers. Letting go of this radiant girl, his hands rested on her shoulders long enough to make certain that she'd stand on her own.

"I couldn't resist that," he said from a dry throat. "Not every day does a lovely girl fall into a man's arms."

Portia was deeply moved by the knowledge that he had some genuine feeling for her in spite of her having apparently made every possible mistake in the pursuit of a man. She wanted to say directly that she hoped to see him again, having always been a poor flirt and unable to keep up the pretense of airy banter. On this occasion she was overwhelmed and the words would not be spoken. She had to remain looking at him for seconds, hoping that he was able to understand the expression on her features.

There was some commotion in the hallway at this juncture and she turned to see Sir Marcus and Lady Kimball entering the room.

Sir Marcus, lean and elegant, was unaware of the feelings between his niece and the family's guest. He advanced to shake hands, the sturdy shoes making a sound against the deep carpet. It was the shoes that had betrayed his presence in advance, permitting Portia to compose herself slightly.

"Good to see you again, Jemmy," the preoccupied host said eagerly.

Lady Kimball, in a well-made turquoise sack dress with a narrow panier, turned away from the typical *bonhomie* of a guest such as Jeremy. An inspection of Portia's features convinced her that the girl had been stirred by his presence, but Lady Kimball felt a moment's reassurance for what she imagined was Dulcie's sake. The foolish country girl had chosen to wear that shabbily cut and ill-fitting dress after all, most likely because it was new. Any possibility that she might thereby capture the stylish Jemmy Newlake on the marriage mart seemed to have disappeared. A spouse might forgive such habiliments, or even a suitor; but not any casual acquaintance.

"I see that you have met my husband's niece," Lady Kimball said, carefully pointing out that Portia was no blood relative of hers. "A charming girl, is she not?"

Portia was aware of the older woman's glacial tones and looked anxiously at Jeremy to measure his response, expecting any partisan of hers to be highly critical on the instant. Jeremy, Lord Newlake, however, merely smiled at Lady Kimball and then back to her. In compensation for the silence, Portia thought she saw him wink very swiftly, as if urging mute calm on her as well.

"Decidedly ravishing," Jeremy said, swinging his glass. (She'd had a moment's apprehension that he would speak of the stolen kiss, but it proved groundless. Nor was that surprising, somehow.) "You should have told me of this lovely young creature, Sir Marcus."

The knight's lady interposed. "Portia is staying with us in London."

"Ah. Inspecting the places of interest, to be sure." He chuckled overlong, winking once again at her. "I have no doubt that your curiosity will find its suitable reward."

Lady Kimball was gratified by what seemed like elaborate indifference on his part. Only Portia realized that Jeremy was skillfully placating Lady Kimball and herself at the same time. If she'd had such talents at diplomacy, which she deeply admired, Lady Kimball would have become her dearest friend in the world and even encouraged a possible match between her and Jeremy.

"As bad luck would have it," Portia's aunt said, "arrangements were made a while ago for this dear girl to be supping elsewhere tonight."

"No," Jeremy said, so quickly it ought to have been plain to any other close observer that he was truly irritated. But he covered the lapse promptly by adding with cool politeness, "I insist that she stay and illuminate the groaning board by her presence."

"You're very kind," Lady Kimball said, implying that Jeremy couldn't have been more courteous to a bedlamite than to Portia. She accepted the peer's true feelings as little more than honeyed flattery. He had made his peace with Lady Kimball far too efficiently, it seemed. "When you next come to see Dulcie, I can assure you that Portia will be with us, if she still remains in London."

"As nothing is certain, from what you yourself say, I insist that she stay to supper tonight and give me the great benefit of her company."

"But Portia has promised to attend the Eastwood *soirée.*"

"The Eastwoods? I will make my apologies to Hartley and Louisa for the inconvenience." Then he drawled, "If any compensation is possible to atone for the absence of so splendid a young female."

Portia never for a moment felt that he was dealing with her as insincerely as with Lady Kimball. His assurance to her lay not so much in an occasional wink as in the sudden uncontrolled changes in his speaking voice, changes which Lady Kimball was momentarily too self-assured to assess or even discern.

Lady Kimball's wits still functioned on a primary level,

however. She turned to Portia and said, "In any case, you must complete your *toilette*, my dear."

Portia understood what her aunt was actually saying. After excusing herself, she could then proceed to the Eastwoods, as had originally been planned. Portia wasn't a deceitful person herself, but she was certainly alive to the deceits of others.

"I relish the young lady's company exactly as she is," Jeremy said airily, having probably sensed what the beldame had planned. "Sir Marcus, perhaps you can persuade these ladies to alter their plans."

"It would be most awkward," the knight said with an apprehensive glance at his wife.

"But not impossible," Jeremy pointed out. "I did you a good turn today and ask for one on your behalf as payment."

The Kimballs understood that Jeremy Newlake had discovered at least one possible contender for the hand of their niece.

Lady Kimball began, "I do think that good manners would require Portia's presence elsewhere on this night."

But she didn't sound as insistent as theretofore. It seemed that Jeremy wanted to have the country mouse's company so that he could make sport of her, which was too wicked of him! But that wasn't the same as seeing some genuine attraction in her, and the difference made Portia's company acceptable if that was necessary.

"When you put it in terms of favors to be returned," the knight responded, understanding from long experience of his wife that her feelings had slightly changed, "it is difficult for another man to refuse."

Lady Kimball promptly addressed herself to the matter of ordering another place set at table. Jeremy, in his role of paying overmuch attention to Portia, escorted her into the huge dining room with its oval table and the full-length mirror on one wall. Portia was deeply unsettled by the touch of his wrist beneath her palm as they walked, and could say nothing. Jeremy spoke innocuously but only after a long silence and in response to some question from the restless Lady Kimball.

Dulcie had, of course, joined them by now, dressed in white poplin to give further accent to her blond hair and crystal-clear skin. She spoke almost entirely to Portia, which disturbed her mother, as a lively conversation was taking place between the males.

During the first course, of lentil soup, Portia noticed that Jeremy's sharp nose looked rather endearing. During the steamed halibut she noticed that his hands moved in talk, a trait that seemed winning to her.

During the chicken, she became aware of his swift looks in her direction, although he had been seated next to Dulcie. Rarely did he address Portia and then only with exaggerated politeness along the lines that Lady Kimball seemed to expect, but the quick and concerned glances told Portia that he was not at all unaware of her presence.

During the roast beef, he ventured on his first witticism of the dinner. Noticing that the lean knight, like himself, was only picking at his food after the numerous preceding courses, an untypical attitude that they shared, Jeremy said, "Apparently, Marcus, you aren't a knight of the dining table, performing prodigious feats at the festive board."

At the conclusion of that play on words, he glanced at Portia to see her response, and was gratified by her laughter. Lady Kimball, who had seen the byplay, spoke sharply to Dulcie and nodded only slightly when her daughter made some vacuous remark to Jeremy, who brushed it away with a smile and a wave of one hand.

Lady Kimball, who believed that persistence was always a virtue, continued to prod Dulcie with looks as the men resumed their conversation. Jeremy paused every so often to swivel his head only partly around so that without facing Portia he could move his eyes in such a way that Portia knew she was being favorably examined once more.

Dulcie, however, didn't have the bold-as-brass temperament to interpose on a conversation that dealt with horses or Parliament on Jeremy's side, and with the Army and his late heroic brother Alisdair when her father introduced a topic.

Without any such reservations herself, Lady Kimball gained the gentlemen's attention by clearing her throat and then said, "Jeremy, I wonder that you can sit at one table with a young woman—two young women, I should say, of course—and talk of nothing but masculine concerns. It shows far less *politesse*, far less refinement, than I would have expected to see in you."

Jeremy forebore to point out that his host had initiated the talk along those lines. "It has been remiss of me, to be sure."

But his first apologetic smile was for Portia.

"One would think," said Lady Kimball pointedly, "that a finely dressed young woman had hardly ever caught your attention."

"Of course I am aware of a female's good points."

"And have been in so many past cases, from what I reliably hear."

"I bow to the gossipmongers, and to Mr. Colburn's novels."

Portia almost called out with surprise. She had read some of the novels that Mr. Henry Colburn's press churned out when not employed on issues of *The Court Journal* or *Atheneum*. She had understood that the characters were thinly veiled portraits of actual members of the *haut ton*, but wouldn't have believed that Jeremy, for one, carried on in such a rakish manner, with so little regard for the sensibilities of others. She supposed that he had been sowing his wild oats, and found herself hoping that the process had been completed by now.

"Then, why are you not aware of the young woman at table

now?" In her eagerness she did not trouble to employ the plural. "Some explanation is surely needed on your part."

"I am most certainly aware of the great charms of Miss Portia here, whom I had the honor of meeting for the first time only a while ago." And he looked directly at her as if to further apologize for the graceless words of his hostess.

"Portia's rural attractions to one side, my dear Jemmy—" Lady Kimball began.

"As for Dulcie," Jeremy added, "having liked her from childhood and been happy to see her own charms developing, she is well aware of my respect and admiration of her manifold virtues."

Dulcie acknowledged these encomiums with a sisterly smile.

Her mother sniffed the air like a hound on the scent. "'Respect and admiration.' I would have expected you to see more in Dulcie, considering how well you know her."

"Those are splendid attitudes to have for another person."

Sir Marcus began to say something about embarrassments, but Lady Kimball wouldn't be swerved from pursuing the point. Even Portia, who hardly knew her aunt, could have told him that the small effort was useless.

"What, then, my dear Jemmy, do you hope for in a young woman? What qualities do you seek in a girl before you would offer for her?"

Asked about his views, Jeremy, who had been sipping his tea, pulled back and considered the matter seriously. "I have found that my life in Parliament and throughout London causes me to see many of both sexes who say one thing and mean another. At parties and routs, in debates, it happens all the time. One adopts a similar manner as a protective coloration. Otherwise it is impossible to thrive in the metropolis. I suppose, then, that I would most value in a female the un-London-like quality of directness. I seek a female who informs a man what her feelings are and why, a girl who is not Janus-faced."

He didn't have to look across at Portia this time. From the start, he must have sensed keenly that her dealings with him had been absolutely to the point. Surely it was miraculous that a girl who found elaborate courtesy agonizingly difficult while admiring it keenly should have encountered a man who appreciated honesty because he was forbidden to practice that one quality.

Lady Kimball, for her part, didn't believe in Jeremy's own spurt of honesty. It seemed likely that he wanted to make somewhat more subtle sport of a clumsy outlander, still pretending he was delighted by her. The male hadn't lived who truly wanted anything from a woman but to be flattered and cosseted and made much of.

"Perhaps," she said neutrally, avoiding the temptation to insist that Dulcie had often been chided maternally for being so direct. He had known Dulcie these many years and wouldn't believe one word of that.

A comical notion had come to Portia's mind while listening. She imagined Lady Kimball informing others about Jeremy's views, and daughters of *ton* then being instructed to irritate and insult Lord Newlake in the good name of feigned directness. The conceit made her chuckle, and she was aware of a brief but poisoned glance from Lady Kimball.

When supper concluded, at eight-thirty, the ladies rose to withdraw. Jeremy, on his feet, made a point of looking into Portia's eyes and speaking quietly.

"I hope that I shall be favored by your company at least once again before you see fit to deprive London of your presence."

"Yes, of course," Portia said instantly, then chuckled her appreciation of the reason for his eyes suddenly glinting. She added demurely, "My hope, Lord Newlake, is no less than yours."

Feeling as if she walked on a cloud, she went to the door. Dulcie, at her side, nodded understandingly, well aware that Portia was taken by her friend of long standing.

Lady Kimball, moving like a stately galleon under full sail, was the last out of the dining room. She waited, hesitating, till she heard her husband say to Jeremy, "I take it, then, that your quest has been successful."

She didn't close the drawing-room door till she had heard Jeremy's confirming response. "Beyond my best expectations it has been successful."

Portia, preceding her to the lower drawing room, was a little surprised on looking back to see that her aunt, despite recent adversities, wasn't bristling with anger. Portia didn't know of Lady Kimball's newly reinforced conviction that by the time Jeremy Newlake again saw Portia, that troublesome young lady would be engaged to some honorable man of a lower station. It bothered Lady Kimball not in the slightest that the young man, no matter how many good points he might boast, couldn't possibly be Portia's very first choice.

CHAPTER 7

It is a truth universally acknowledged that any young lady who hopes to be romantically involved very soon must be in want of a *confidante*. No matter what the other girl's feelings, the smitten one feels that her pleasures and uncertainties must be communicated to another.

Portia and Dulcie were ensconced in Dulcie's room, with its oriental-inspired trumpery that was chockablock from ceiling to floor. On this bright May morning of the next day, Portia had already spoken of her burgeoning depth of feeling for Jeremy Newlake. Dulcie, as it fortunately transpired, showed genuine pleasure at the prospects that loomed for her cousin. She went on to speak of Jeremy's family estate at Lavenham, in East Anglia, where his spinster sister and ever-tired mother chose to stay all year long. Seeing her cousin's restiveness while she offered the admirable figures about Jeremy's yearly income, Dulcie returned to the original subject of their collective cogitations and expressed hope that Jeremy shared fully in this onset of affection.

Portia was on the point of hopeful agreement when Humility, Lady Kimball's maid, knocked respectfully on the portal.

"Lady Kimball asks that you both go downstairs to greet Mr. Lionel," the maid announced.

"My brother," Dulcie said to Portia. "You haven't met him yet."

"I look forward to doing so."

A morning is generally enlived by some new arrival, but in the Kimball establishment at this time everyone but Portia was thrown into a fit of depression or stifled anger. Dulcie's brother had returned from the country one day late, which angered Lady Kimball. Further, Lionel Kimball made a point of saying that he would have liked to remain in Herefordshire forever, which depressed Sir Marcus and Dulcie alike.

As to Portia, who entered the drawing room for the ostensible purpose of meeting her cousin, she found herself witnessing the last minutes of a family argument. Lady Kimball looked at her after almost every sally, as if expecting Portia to take her aunt's side. This she stubbornly refused to do, but seated herself, with reluctance, as none of the family apparently wanted her to leave.

Lionel Kimball, at twenty-one, was a picture of dejection. Although he had inherited his father's slimness and features, the latter had been darkened with liberal applications of sun. He kept his eyes riveted gloomily to the floor, having welcomed wordlessly one more auditor of this tragic scene.

"I am aware of the range of your interests, and that they are limited to a farm," Lady Kimball was saying as Portia seated herself and was the object of a brisk glance from her aunt. "But you are at home now."

"I don't want to be." Lionel shrugged wearily. He was a young man who would not be cured of gloom and would partake sadly in any revel. Portia could tell after only one long look at him.

"You haven't the choice."

Lionel glanced at his father, somehow thinking after more than two decades that Sir Marcus had some actual voice in an important matter. "I could spend two years as an estate agent and, with my abilities proven, purchase a farm to cultivate. And then I would marry."

Sir Marcus was affronted, genuinely, by such a program. "If you must have an active career, the Army would certainly be available to you. Your uncle Alisdair knew it was the best vocation in the world for any young man so misguided that he absolutely insists on keeping busy."

"The Army would prevent him from marriage in the *haut,* just as much as if he had been born to a barbary ape," Lady Kimball snapped, not for the first time, as Portia was certain. The argument was a long-standing one, which it was possible to tell from the determined whine in every voice. "At any rate, you are home to stay and on pain of your parents' displeasure you will behave like a London-born and -bred gentleman."

Firmly convinced for the moment that she had made her point beyond cavil, Lady Kimball walked out of the drawing room.

Sir Marcus joined her after a while, which left Portia alone with brother and sister. Lionel emerged from his comatose state only when informed that his cousin hailed from farm country in Sussex, and Portia had to remind him that hops were grown in the area along with pigs and sturdy oak.

By the time he had conveyed to Portia and his sister that he was unlikely to attempt suicide at least until after supper, Lionel indicated that he would soon be off somewhere or other. Dulcie riposted that he was probably going to the embankment to farm the dirt. The young man, still dispirited, sidled out the door. Dulcie was more than ready to give consideration to another matter of moment.

"A ride in the park will be splendid for this afternoon," she said, her skin glowing in anticipation. "We will take the vis-à-vis carriage and see the dandies. And they, in turn, will see us."

It hardly mattered that Portia was disinclined to shop among the youthful gentry of *le monde.* Dulcie was anxious to leave and couldn't attend by herself. That drawback was sufficient to bring Portia to her side.

Attired in a royal blue day dress, a lightly weighted pelisse, and a pink-trimmed bonnet, she joined Dulcie at the appointed hour. Their taciturn coachman drove under the sunny cloudless sky. Portia had time to look briefly at the Serpentine and decide that she wasn't actually sure whether or not the grass at home, as she still thought of Sussex, was greener. It seemed important that she couldn't make up her mind in the matter.

She looked much longer at the Rotten Row sand track. Puffed and powdered dandies were on horses or in carriages, and some, afoot, strode the area. A remark was made at every passing female and more than one ninnyhammer seemed to look out from a vis-à-vis and chuckle in return. Dulcie managed to seem disapproving and inviting at the same time, a fine art mastered by every female since Eve.

Portia, who had entertained the notion that Jeremy might be somewhere on the premises, found herself hoping that he hadn't been there in many months.

When they had passed the young men, Dulcie smiled at her companion. "Shall we give them once more the inestimable benefits of our company?"

Portia couldn't help making a face.

"After a few moments, of course," Dulcie said kindly. "It will seem as if we are coming back from our ride, which we must do, and I am certain the *pourparlers* will amuse you in time."

Footpaths had been laid out on either side of the Row, and the coachman swung across one of these to prepare for a turnaround that wouldn't look as if it had been intended from the start.

This practical gesture had the effect of disconcerting a male and female who were walking arm in arm. The young man, having protected his escort by interposing himself between her and the vehicle, turned to glare at it; then his eyes widened briefly and his lips crinkled down at the corners, as if the worst possible circumstance had overtaken him.

It was the unwonted sadness in the young man's demeanor that caused Portia to look keenly at him. Her surprise was short in duration. Although he was with a young lady, Lionel Kimball contrived to look as if his dog had just died hideously.

Portia, feeling a moment's good-hearted concern in spite of her former perceptions of the young man's character, said, "Something terrible must have happened!"

"Not to Lionel, only to those around him of a good disposition." Dulcie acted to soothe her cousin's generous concern. She directed the coachman to stop a dozen feet off and await their return.

"Come with me, Portia, and you shall hear how dire is the peril." Dulcie laughed.

With parasols unfurled, the young ladies stepped daintily along the footpath. Twenty paces were enough to bring on a confrontation of the girls with Duclie's fallen-faced brother.

Dulcie suggested puckishly, "You are so sad because nothing is wrong."

"Much," answered Lionel with the dignity of a French aristocrat seeing the tumbril from a corner of an eye, "is wrong."

"Nothing immediate, I mean. What I wish to prove to Portia is that nothing has gone cataclysmically wrong in the last (shall we say?) three minutes."

"Of course it has." Lionel sounded irritable, as if it would have been foolish to expect anything else in a matter that concerned him.

"Would you care to enlighten us, dear brother of mine? It will not, of course, be for attribution."

Lionel glanced doubtfully at Portia, who was amused in spite of herself by what must certainly have been an excessively lugubrious manner even for him.

"I have never been tortured by someone using wild horses, Cousin Lionel, but if those were employed to gain a confidence of yours, I would hold my tongue to the last."

Such words meant little to the distracted Lionel. He had, however, remembered one high point on her *dossier* as it had been given to him earlier, and decided to communicate his woes when in the company of a farm maid. "The girl I wish to marry has—"

"To marry?" Now Dulcie did look startled. "Well, I know that you have been mooning about for these last few months, but I had no idea that nuptials were in the offing."

"Nor do we," Lionel murmured so quietly that Portia didn't hear the words.

"Forgive me," she said, "but when two people decide upon marriage, it is considered a happy occasion. About what may happen afterwards I cannot venture a comment, but the first moments are intended to be filled with joy."

"Not for us."

"Naturally not," Dulcie said, but her tone was slightly less reserved. She was now prepared to show concern if the forthcoming revelations warranted it. "May we ask what is the difficulty?"

"I cannot leave London to follow my vocation."

"Does your bride-to-be wish you to leave?"

"Like myself, she desires to be quit of London more than of anyplace else in the world."

He had been standing in front of the girl, but now she moved to his right and faced the inquisitors. A sensibly dressed young woman of Portia's age, red-haired and with fair skin—and well-spoken, as she now proved. "We have not met heretofore," she said quietly and shyly. "My name is Faye Amphrey."

"How do you do?" Portia responded instantly, trying with all the warmth of her nature to put the other at ease. "I do congratulate my cousin Lionel for inveigling you into marriage. I hope he proves worthy of you, but I entertain my doubts."

Faye Amphrey smiled and cast down her eyes with becoming modesty.

Dulcie, who had been deep in thought, considered that gesture, so uncharacteristic in a young female conversing with others, and said, "I am not familiar with the surname and take it that you are not of *ton*."

Faye Amphrey shook her head mutely without looking up.

Portia and Dulcie exchanged glances, each silently communicating the knowledge that Lady Kimball would immediately see to it that the banns were forbidden.

Faye Amphrey cleared her throat. "My family is perfectly respectable and—and honorable and decent. Only, I am never allowed to forget that my father is—I blush to confess it—a mere laborer."

Portia couldn't believe that any laborer's daughter would be so fine-spoken. A good education was costly.

"What form of labor does he practice?"

"It horrifies me to tell you."

"He is not in the armed force, because such a vocation would hardly drive others to outright disapproval. Nor, to judge from your accents, is he a blacksmith or bricklayer."

"It would not change matters if he were."

Portia forebore to dispute that point from the father's view. "What type of labor does he perform, then, that keeps your family out of the best society?"

Faye looked around to make sure that no one would overhear, then confessed her deepest family shame: "He is a . . . a banker."

Portia felt that an honorable working man with a good income (or even without) need apologize to no one, and Mr. Amphrey's nearest and dearest were plainly not being kept in a state of deprivation. This was no time, however, to offer consolations that wouldn't actually console.

Dulcie pursed her lips. Unlike Portia, she knew the full extent of that silken persecution which must have been Faye Amphrey's portion in London, with an affluent family in which one of the members worked.

"I'll never be permitted to forget the humiliation, as it's

considered here, as long as I stay in this city," Faye pursued sadly. "And I would leave on the moment to marry Lionel, but I cannot do so and neither can he."

Dulcie said, "A pretty dilemma," but sounded more sympathetic than she had done up to this point.

Portia, feeling guilty for having previously made some mild sport of the powerfully unhappy Lionel, looked with a certain keenness at the young couple.

"If I follow this development correctly, you both would be happier on a farm such as I came from."

"Yes, but it's an idle dream," Lionel said, speaking for both. Faye was content to nod her agreement.

The idea came to Portia as soon as the words passed her lips: "It doesn't have to be a dream."

Lionel, of course, shook his head at the first proffered hope.

Faye, more alert, asked with eagerness, "Have you evolved a stratagem?"

"Quite so. My uncle, Stanley Galton, owns a farm near the town of Hove, in Sussex. He is not a gentleman farmer. He needs others who will help in the day-to-day work and the management of his lands. Tell him who you are and that I'm the one who suggested you. If your work is suitable, I feel sure that you can keep a berth with him until you are prepared to acquire a holding of your own."

Lionel had looked up. It would be too much to say that he was hopeful, but he seemed willing to postpone suicide for several moments at the least.

Faye said, "This is very good of you."

"Not at all. It is my dear uncle who will have to bear the brunt of your affianced's peculiar humors."

She said quietly, "If we are both in a better place, we will be happy."

Dulcie did not make the pejorative comment that soared to her lips. "Discuss it together and lay your plans," she said, looking at her brother and only then at Faye. Despite her railley, she retained considerable affection for the lachrymose sibling.

As Portia turned and Dulcie followed, it was possible to hear Lionel and Faye drawing nearer and she guessed that they were embracing. Perhaps their lips touched in a flurry of passion.

Despite the pair's momentary lightening of gloom, Portia admitted to herself that she remained sorry for them. Obstacles in their lives had yet to be conquered. On the other hand, in her case and Jeremy's, their path was clear. Nothing at all stood in the way of happiness, and she awaited with keen anticipation her next meeting with the man who would make her happy forever.

CHAPTER 8

The girls proceeded silently to Jermyn Street without even a brief interlude for Dulcie to exchange witticisms with a few of the dandies in Hyde Park. At home, Dulcie was requested to join Lady Kimball in the downstairs drawing room, and Portia went up to take her rest before supper.

Such ease was short-lived on this occasion. Dulcie hurried into the room, fresh excitement pinking her cheeks.

"We are to attend a party on this very night," she burst out upon entering. "The decision to that effect was made only minutes ago."

"It will be *haut ton,* I presume?"

"Not at all, I am myself surprised to say. The founder of the feast is Colonel Rupert Duggin, of the Seventh Foot."

"If the affair is not *ton,* I wonder that the family will attend."

"We are to make at least a brief appearance for sweet sentiment's sake. Colonel Duggin, you see, was an Army colleague and great friend of my late heroic uncle, Colonel Alisdair Kimball. Colonel Duggin, however, survived the battles in America, thereby being forced to give occasional parties and attend others so as to indulge in necessary social activities which he finds rather distasteful."

"For such an occasion, then, my wardrobe is suitable, even by my aunt's exalted standards."

"Better to be dressed in the fashion," Dulcie pointed out indisputably. "In which case, you must perforce borrow one of my gowns."

"My aunt will be angry."

"That is her right, if she wishes to exercise it." Dulcie tossed her head spiritedly, having had much time to recall how effectively Portia had proved that the minotaur could be thwarted. "I will handle that difficulty when and if it arises. Meanwhile, we must proceed to my room, where we can rig you."

"It is the fit that remains in question," Portia remarked as the two girls entered that simulacrum of the fabled Orient which was Dulcie's quarters.

"White is, of course, the universal color," Dulcie ruminated needlessly. "A bright-haired girl like myself looks well in it, a dark-haired girl like you certainly does, and so would a carrot-haired girl like Faye. I need hardly tell you that I kept my peace about the matter of Lionel and Faye whilst I was closeted with my Mamma. Indeed I wonder how soon—"

"Best not to discuss it here," Portia said, reminding herself and Dulcie of Lady Kimball's habit of materializing unheard when she chose to do so.

Dulcie agreed wordlessly. Having consulted some unseen oracle in the pause that followed, she reached for a gown.

"To our muttons now, Portia! Try this on yourself."

Portia obliged. The dress was of white-striped bombazine with banded sleeves. Warily, she touched the cleavage, which was a bit more than young ladies showed at routs back in Hove.

"I feel certain our Dilys can repair that in secret by the use of a bib, Portia, if you wish," Dulcie said comfortingly. She must have been referring to the family seamstress, one of the retainers whom Portia had not yet encountered. "Given a small tuck here in the gown, and a slighty larger tuck there, by London standards your rig-out will look only mildly imperfect."

Portia made a face.

"But it will reflect your spirit," Dulcie said in a different and far more amiable tone of voice. "It will be quite lovely."

The family berline, with four glossy bays in front and two footmen behind and a coachman muffling his yawns, proceeded down Clifford Street. Lady Kimball, her mostly unlined skin pale above a dark pelisse, had spent many silent moments glaring at Portia in her daughter's white bombazine. Portia smiled back once and then closed her eyes, hoping that she appeared unconcerned and not angry at being made a pariah for dressing in the current fashion.

Lady Kimball glared in turn at her daughter. Dulcie looked uncomfortable at first and then shrugged with difficulty. Lady Kimball's eyes narrowed in fury. Dulcie, feeling rebuked, managed to keep her upper lip from quivering fearfully, which had been her usual response to such provocation in the past. There was still a wary regard for Mamma, which seemed, most times, quite proper. Portia, smiling encouragingly at her cousin, decided that Dulcie would become a full-fledged rebel only if something important to her was involved.

At this point Lady Kimball, having seen Portia's glance over at Dulcie, glowered disapprovingly at her. The older woman assumed that the niece's example had bred lawlessness in the daughter. In this she was, of course, quite correct.

Only one male had joined them, and it wasn't Dulcie's brother. Lionel had not been at home, and so the others left without the inestimable benefit of his companionship. Sir Marcus, in a cloak that hid most of a long-tailed coat and yellow pantaloons, tapped his palms repeatedly against the tasseled Hessian boots that it suited him to wear.

It was Sir Marcus who coughed and thereby shattered the long silence. Portia was the only other who seemed free of some stress, and so he conferred his attentions upon her.

"This is your debut London party," he said pleasantly, articulating the first words that came to mind. "I'm glad to see you looking so well turned out for the occasion."

He was aware of some noise like a hissing snake, but couldn't credit the notion that a serpent might somehow have entered a berline carriage on a London street. His wife's lips were slightly parted, though, and he presumed that the sound had come from that source. If Sir Marcus hadn't known Beatrice as well as he did, the idea would have occurred to him that she was in some way irritated.

The *feu de joie* which they would attend was apparently being held in New Burlington Street. Upon descending from the carriage, their way was lit by a torch-carrying linkboy, so-called, who looked to be in his sixties.

Colonel Duggin's residence was a three-story home with molded doors and square windows. From the front steps to some point out of sight, the establishment was chockablock with humanity. Most of the men wore Army uniforms suitable for parading: scarlet coats with white crossbelts and white duck trousers. The females, it lightly occurred to Portia, found greater variety in their uniforms.

She proceeded inside with the Kimballs. In a far-off room, with carved brocade-seat chairs against the walls, was a sideboard with comestibles. Wine and whiskey were among the delicacies and even the green tea that was mockingly known as Regent's Punch. Dancing had been halted, most likely for a brief time. Sir Marcus turned to greet their host, Colonel Duggin, who smiled back nervously. The colonel didn't stoop to Lionel's congenital sadness at being in such a social situation, but he was not prepared to shout with happiness, either.

Sir Marcus eventually rejoined the three females. The sight of so much military plumage had apparently distracted him. "I've always thought that my brother was made happier by the Army uniforms than by opportunities for heroics. If anybody had told me that Alisdair of all men would become a hero, I'd have laughed merrily."

Lady Kimball, who had heard all this in the past, was irritable. "We will let you know when leaving here becomes suitable. In the meantime, you can go into some other room and trade on your brother's reputation."

Sir Marcus recognized that his wife was tense and availed himself of the opportunity.

Lady Kimball, looking around, was surprised to see several notables. Little Rees Gronow was disporting himself and so was the ugly but noble-natured Will Alvanley. She thought she saw the first Baron of Restormel in the crowd. Presumably these men, like the Kimballs, would make a brief appearance and then depart for greener pastures.

Her eyes were fixed on a handsome, steel-backed young man who approached and turned to Portia.

"You, Miss, have been pointed out to me as Portia Galton."

"Indeed." On the briefest possible acquaintance, Portia found herself irritated by his assumption that she wouldn't dare not to be Miss Galton.

"Your appearance is not displeasing to me."

"How gratifying," Portia murmured, astonished by this corruption of mannerly behavior that must have been accepted the world over—except in the Army, or so it seemed.

"I was informed that you are comely, but also that you haven't become used to our London ways."

Portia had determined that she wouldn't have anything to do with this arrogant and condescending popinjay. Courtesy, whether from a Londoner or a denizen of Sussex, demanded that she show sufficient coolness for him to understand that he need make no attempt to further the acquaintance.

"I am happy for the qualified praise, but not able to see how it affects you, sir."

He was more struck by the impersonal word than by the

tone. "I am Ivor Turbayne," said this manifestation. "Lieutenant—one of many, I must add—in the Seventh Foot."

If she had been feeling friendlier, Portia might have made some hopefully amusing remark about the other six feet. As it was, she merely looked away. It would have been impossible to show her indifference more plainly.

Ivor Turbayne remained wholly unfazed. He assumed that the gel was merely being coquettish in the style of female outlanders. His steely eyes met Lady Kimball's.

"I will dance with Miss Galton and return her to you once the next quadrille is completed."

Portia spoke before her aunt could respond, most likely, judging by her smile, with agreement. "But I, sir, will not dance with you."

The repeated "sir" ought to have been the last deadly insult, causing him to withdraw hastily. Portia had not, however, reckoned with the fabled persistence of the military.

Rather than take his *congé* with alacrity, the lieutenant became irritable. "I will not permit this behavior."

"How fortunate that you can decide in advance on the permissible attitudes of others."

In his muffled anger, the young officer's normally deep voice was lowered even further. "This is not the way to begin a long friendship with me."

"Quite true. It is the way to keep any such hideous error from being made."

Lieutenant Turbayne seemed to puff himself up till Portia wondered whether or not his midsection would give way with fury. He was a very handsome man, one of those rare males whose features and posture draw the admiration of females and the envy of men. Steely-eyed, ramrod-straight, tall, he resembled nothing human as much as he resembled a figure in some romantical novel from Mr. Colburn's press. Those perfect attributes had changed his life, making him a likely candidate for some showy preferment. With an Army commission purchased by his late parents' spending most of the father's hard-earned savings, he had come to believe in the heroic image of himself that was held by others. On occasion he argued that the Regent ought to send forces back to reconquer America, adding that he would be among the first to volunteer for such an expedition to remove the smirch from Bulldom's escutcheon. Only a hardened cynic would have pointed out that Ivor Turbayne knew nothing of such a fray at first hand, having been too young in '12 for active service.

In response to Portia's finally unmistakable expression of distaste, he showed astonishment. Plainly he was not accustomed to having a female speak to him in this wise, and sought for the unkindest retort that was in him.

"Not even a splendid dowry can make me consent to the desired arrangement."

He was now prepared to leave, fancying that he had punctured her vanity with a verbal *epée* thrust. Portia was so startled that she spoke to him.

"How do you mean those words?"

"Your biddable qualities were exaggerated to me and I was assured that you would be happy to wed a man of my prospects and would relish being a good and obedient wife to a masterful male."

"You were told this?" In spite of her best efforts to keep control of her manner, Portia's cheeks flamed. She knew now why the elder Kimballs had stooped to attend this far-from-*ton* assemblage, as it offered an opportunity for her to meet the lout for whom they intended her. It was difficult to know whether she felt angry or amused. "May I ask who confided to you these secrets of my heart?"

"Sir Marcus reassured me of your qualities just now, when Colonel Duggin introduced me to him." Turbayne was paying little attention to the gel's words. Instead he was ventilating his grievance while attempting to rouse regret in her bosom for having rejected his manly advances. Probably she had not expected to make a life with a strong leader and been thrown into some sort of fit by the prospect. "But it was the representative of the family, the one who first spoke to me yesterday (was it?) at Stephen's Hotel in Bond Street, then requested me to wait upon him at his chambers, who was the most impressive: He discussed your good qualities very earnestly. I may add that he mentioned the substantial dowry and thereby aroused my keen interest in the splendid traits that were so trenchantly described to me."

"Who was this person, this fount of information?" Portia glanced from the corner of an eye at her aunt, who had almost certainly uncorked the bottle that held such an evil djinn. Lady Kimball was too far off to hear the exchanges, and unwilling to risk Portia's possibly vocal disapproval by drawing closer.

"Why, he was a man of rank and who we can all respect." Having surprised Portia, he now shocked her. "I refer to Jeremy, Lord Newlake."

Portia's astonishment knew no bounds. She gasped, her jaw falling. Most of a minute had passed, long enough for the dancers to begin the *la trenise* figure of this quadrille, before she was able to speak.

"Then, sir, I suggest that you plight your troth with Jeremy Newlake, as he impresses you so sincerely."

Lady Kimball discerned from Portia's face that no progress would be made for a while and that she was cold to reason. There could be no further excuse for remaining where the lesser classes chose to congregate.

She was industriously rising to her feet, and therefore missed the look that suddenly passed from Dulcie to Lieutenant Turbayne's classic features.

"We will be leaving now," said Lady Kimball with authority.

CHAPTER 9

The ride home to Jermyn Street was made longer because the berline carriage was populated by four people wholly absorbed in their own thoughts. Sir Marcus, who had finally been collected for a reluctant departure, was thinking of the military life with its calls to action and wondering again how his mediocrity of a brother, Alisdair, had been able to distinguish himself by dying a hero's death.

Dulcie, too, was considering a military personage, but a younger one. Indeed a smile came to her lips at memory of the godlike Lieutenant Turbayne.

Lady Kimball for her part was making plans to discuss Portia's behavior with her at another time. Certainly Portia must be brought to see that a handsome man with an income, however small, was a desirable catch and better by far than might fall to her portion if she stayed in that Sussex village from which she had been brought to *le monde,* probably by main force.

As for Portia, the sustained bitterness of her thoughts make it desirable to draw the veil of charity over them. Let it suffice to say that she felt betrayed but wouldn't divert Lady Kimball by publicly bursting into tears.

The silent foursome arrived in the *purlieus* of Jermyn Street at long last. Portia, with only the most perfunctory farewells, repaired to her room. Wholly ignoring the possibility of illumination, she removed the borrowed dress and then tumbled into bed, raising the quilt modestly over her torso and up to the neck.

Not even in the privacy of this room did the opportunity
arise immediately for tears. There was a series of discreet
knocks against the door panel. Portia remained silent, briefly
wishing that she was a university male who could have
sported his oak to indicate an unwillingness to countenance
any interruption. There was a pause and then the door was
opened by someone who must have been impatient.

"Portia, aren't you here?" Dulcie's voice sounded pettish for
once.

Silence would have caused the other to leave. But she did
owe Dulcie a great debt for kindnesses rendered. As Dulcie
was anxious to talk, Portia damped down her own unhappiness and made herself available for consultations.

"Come in, pray do."

Dulcie asked no questions about the reason for staying in
darkness so early. Instead she lit the wax candle on the table
and replaced the metal lighter rod in its toy pagoda. Only
then did she close the door. Her walk was slow, making
hardly any sound. As Portia watched, she seated herself on
the claw-legged chair with its brocade pillow. The room's yellow wallpaper by candlelight gave an oriental cast to her skin,
but paradoxically whitened her bright blond hair.

Portia expected to hear some comment about the inad-
visability of taking to bed so early, and possibly even a concerned query about her state of health. She need not have
given thought to this matter. Dulcie was preoccupied with
her own feelings and nothing else.

"He is the most beautiful man I ever saw," she gushed,
speaking quietly at Portia's gesture in order to keep Lady
Kimball from making one of those infamous surprising en-
trances of hers. Now that Portia was in the room and available for discourse, Dulcie was pleasant in temper. "A prince
among men, truly."

Portia, in no mood whatever to hear anyone singing the

praises of the opposite sex, kept that feeling to herself as well. "Might I ask to whom you refer?"

"Lieutenant Turbayne, of course." And, in a thrilled hush, "Ivor. Isn't that the most beautiful name? And it suits him so! Lieutenant Ivor Turbayne."

It was clear that Dulcie, like Portia an aeon ago, was in desperate need of a *confidante* to whom she could reveal the secrets of her heart.

"Are you telling me that you have been smitten by Lieutenant Turbayne?"

"Yes. And I think, Portia, that he is smitten with me." Dulcie hugged her knees in a recollection of pleasure. "He looked at me just before we left the party, and I could see his feelings written large upon that splendid face."

There was no accounting for tastes, Portia decided. If a girl of sense could be enchanted by a great dolt like Turbayne, then it was little wonder that so many were driven distracted by the game of hearts.

"Isn't he the most magnificent man you have ever seen?" Dulcie pursued, wanting an admission of how much she was to be envied.

"He is very handsome, assuredly," Portia said in all truth.

"And that godlike, decisive male is the one who will offer for me. He could not be interested in you any longer, even though Mamma apparently intended him to be." Dulcie's chin was set firmly, and if any other person had told her that she was strong-willed by nature she would have been skeptical. "I don't know by what necromancy Mama will be made to consent to my nuptials with Ivor, but consent she will."

"I most assuredly wish you the best of fortune in this endeavor."

"Thank you, dear Portia, for being kind. It is no more than a girl in love would expect from you."

Some shadow of personal feeling must have passed unwittingly across Portia's face. Dulcie drew a deep breath of surprise, because reality as perceived by someone else had intruded upon these girlish maunderings.

"I am terribly sorry for you, Portia," she added in a different tone of voice. "Never before did I know Jemmy Newlake to be cruel. First he puts you in his power, so to say, and then arranges to toss you into the arms of another."

Portia was unable to speak about her own difficulties.

"I will leave now, and give you the peace that you want. I hope that you'll feel better tomorrow."

She blew out the wax candle and closed her cousin's door softly.

Portia lay back in bed. Quietly, so as not to draw Lady Kimball's unwanted attention. She cried.

Dulcie had slept on her problem all night, and in the morning decided upon the first step to be taken. It required being assured beyond question that her feelings for Ivor Turbayne were reciprocated. An understanding had to be reached between them as soon as possible. True, they had not even officially been introduced, but she had observed his responses as keenly as she had felt her own.

So how was she to see him again, and quickly? This apparently formidable difficulty, once posed, was soon answered. Ivor would probably join many other officers at Hyde Park, and she would proceed there. It was going to be necessary for her to do it unescorted. Portia's company would not be pleasing to the officer after last night's barbed encounter. As for asking a mere friend to accompany her, the ensuing gossip could do great harm to her cause by reaching Mamma's ears too soon. By herself, then, she would be successful.

Dulcie's twelve o'clock repast was brief, and shared only by Lady Kimball. As might be expected, Mamma knew the whereabouts of everyone in the establishment.

"Father is visiting the Marylebone Cricket Club," she began, not seeing the slightest harm in proving once more that she kept an eye out. "Portia, after her disgraceful behavior of last night, simply declines to have any converse with me or anyone else and is immured in her room. So, presumably, is Lionel in his."

Dulcie didn't see that any blame attached to her cousin for being desirous of privacy at this stage of her affairs.

"And what are your plans for the day, now that you have arisen?" Lady Kimball asked.

"I am to meet Hypatia Innis at her parents' home," Dulcie lied.

"That will be suitable for a few hours. It is also a fact that there is a brother, I believe, and perhaps he would be won over by your charms."

She attired herself in a day dress, pelisse, silk slippers, and poke bonnet in various shades of blue, then carried a white silk parasol. By promising to return at five o'clock, she was able to commandeer the vis-à-vis and a coachman. The trip through those sections of Hyde Park that were likely to be infested with officers was brief in duration but thorough. Ivor, as she thought of Lieutenant Turbayne, had not made himself available to the other girls. She dared to feel certain that the reason lay in his being smitten with her.

She was in no mood to return home without accomplishing the task which she had set herself, and promptly issued another direction to the coachman.

"Go to Stephen's Hotel and ride by it very slowly indeed."

The order was followed, permitting her to see officers in their red-and-white dress uniforms topped by bearskin caps with short red plumes. She did not see Ivor.

"Ride quickly around the block and come back," she instructed, hoping that the gods would permit an encounter between herself and Ivor as if by accident. On this occasion, too, the gods were decidedly unhelpful.

"Let us wait opposite the entrance," she said at last, knowing better than to provoke scandal by entering the premises.

While the coachman looked longingly in the direction of the establishment known as Gentleman Jackson's Boxing Saloon, along Bond Street, Dulcie resisted taking even one glance toward Lady Emma Hamilton's former residence at Number 150. Instead she looked out fixedly at the hotel front. By four-thirty, Ivor had not been in or out.

It needed considerable strength of character to firmly decide upon repeating these actions the next day and until she saw and spoke with him. Dulcie and her dear cousin were both suffering cruelly in the game of hearts, and she felt certain that in neither case would such adversity be allowed to continue.

CHAPTER 10

Vindication for Dulcie's point of view came indirectly, and not because of anything that she did. She was not even at home by a quarter to five, when the significant discovery was made.

It came about because of Lady Kimball's usual late-afternoon ritual, which consisted of reminding herself where everyone in the family could be located. Of Dulcie's whereabouts she felt that she was aware. Sir Marcus had returned from Marylebone earlier than he would have preferred, because he had promised to put his dear wife's mind at ease by doing so. Portia, who could be accounted for a while as part of the family, remained in her room. Lady Kimball knew this because she had heard the girl moving about and occasionally sighing. Not till Portia emerged in a state of anticipatory dread at being criticized would Lady Kimball fulfill the girl's worst expectations, thereby planting the knife of shame a little deeper in that recalcitrant carcass. Lionel, however, had not come to the surface at all, nor had she been aware of any stirrings in his room.

Offered an excuse to thrust herself into someone else's life, she accepted with alacrity. Swiftly she strode up to Lionel's chamber and opened the door without warning. Lady Kimball had previously overruled Mr. Walsh Porter himself to have the room decorated in dark wallpaper, and put in a fireplace with engraved figures, two satinwood chairs, and a claw-footed desk regarded by all as hideous. More to the point was the large bed, which had not been slept in. Advancing concernedly across the multicolored Wilton carpet, Lady Kimball discerned notepaper on the pillow. She reached for it and read wide-eyed what was written there.

The message understood, Lady Kimball took the paper with her and proceeded swiftly downstairs.

Sir Marcus was ensconced in his library, but had chosen to avoid any of the books in his four-panel bookcase and was immersing himself in a newspaper article headed: Can Bonaparte Be Held Securely on Saint Helena?

Lady Kimball distracted her husband from this educational fare by making a loud and pointed remark upon entering. "There is news of which you must be told immediately."

"Well?"

"Lionel has decamped." She very nearly used the word "fled," for some reason of which she wasn't aware.

"How do you know?" asked Sir Marcus, determined to be absolutely sure of the facts before responding to a mere statement.

In reply, Lady Kimball flourished the note. Sir Marcus held it out to the proper arm's length for him to read.

"He has run off to become a farmer." It was a shock despite the knowledge of Lionel's oft-proclaimed tastes. "And he speaks of marriage to follow. Hmm! I had hoped for better from the boy."

"Worse yet, his absence will soon be known all over London."

Sir Marcus noted his dear wife's distress, but misinterpreted the reasons for it. "Over England, you mean! I will see to it that the matter is communicated to the gazettes and the authorities, so Lionel will soon be returned."

"It would then cause a scandal with which we'd be pilloried," Lady Kimball said firmly. "We have raised a son we are unable to control and everyone will know it."

The optimism which was so great a part of this knight's character once again bobbed to the surface.

"I'll see to it that friends in the Army track him down

secretly. We do have reliable friends in that station of life, thanks to Alisdair's surprising heroism before his death in battle."

"If one person gossips, then all precautions will have been useless."

"I'm sure that wouldn't be so among Army men," Sir Marcus began, blindly loyal to the service whose members he admired.

Lady Kimball interrupted. "For the sake of Dulcie's future in the marriage market, we must not take any chance. No one can think that Dulcie comes from a family with one member who is in any way tainted."

Sir Marcus justified a pause to collect his thoughts by drawing a pinch from his gold-edged snuffbox. Having satisfactorily sneezed and then touched a cambric to his nostrils, he was prepared at last to offer a conclusion.

"Lionel took enough of the needful with him, or so his note says," Sir Marcus ruminated. "In which case, he can provide for himself until the moment when he reaches his destination. It is one source of worry removed, and I always did credit Lionel with common sense."

"You do see the bright side," his wife remarked tonelessly.

"But it is disturbing," Sir Marcus added surprisingly. "Damme, Beatrice, but it is deeply disturbing that he felt he could not find his heart's desires with our help."

"We gave him everything a lad might want and he runs off," said Lady Kimball, viewing the problem differently. "In truth, this shows a lack of gratitude that it is painful to contemplate."

Each was still, lost in thoughts long enough for Sir Marcus to repeat his actions with the snuffbox. So shaken was Lady Kimball that for the second time in a row she failed to reproach him for indulging a filthy habit at home.

"There is perforce only one thing to be done," Lady Kimball said at last. "That is to tell everyone he has left with our approval."

"But he hasn't—oh, I see. For Dulcie's sake, you mean. For the sake of her chances at getting a good match."

"Exactly, Marcus." She was in the mood to offer some petty observation about the quickness of his intelligence, but refrained. She had grown fond of him over the years, even though he hadn't been her first choice for a marriage partner, and didn't want to seem eternally waspish in her husband's eyes.

"Very well," Sir Marcus agreed dolefully. "If you'll pardon me, m'dear, after supper I think I shall make my way out to White's and forget these domestic troubles by a little roystering with my betters."

"That is going to be impossible," Lady Kimball informed him. "We are due to go out tonight and must do so, as a way of showing that all is as usual in the family. Further, it will be a good time to put about the story of Lionel's departure for greener fields, so to say, with our complete blessing."

"Well, I suppose you're right."

"Indeed I am."

The events of the ensuing hour served to convince Lady Kimball that every youth on the premises of Jermyn Street had taken leave either of the establishment or of the senses. Dulcie, most affable of daughters, returned home with no more life in her than one of Lord Elgin's Grecian marbles as displayed at Burlington House. She merely nodded upon being told of her brother's recent actions, then drifted up to her room without a word.

Shortly before supper, Humility, Lady Kimball's personal maid, appeared in the downstairs drawing room with a message from her.

"Miss Dulcie presents her respects and declines to partake of supper," the maid announced. "Miss Dulcie has retired for the night."

"She has not," Lady Kimball snapped. "Inform Miss Dulcie that she must present herself here on pain of her parents' displeasure."

It was a weary and drawn daughter who soon joined them. Dulcie sat without asking permission, and was closing her eyes before Lady Kimball spoke.

"You are aware that your father has contrived to obtain an invitation for us tonight to Almack's for one of their Wednesday night *soirées*," Lady Kimball pointed out with a voice that could have been used for waking the dead. "For the sake of your future and the need to convince all that we are not disturbed by your brother's outrageous behavior, of which I will speak to you in time, you must attend."

"I am far too tired to sparkle, Mamma." Dulcie was wholly interested in this event. She had attended Almack's and enjoyed it in the past, but knew perfectly well that Ivor Turbayne lacked the position in society to make an appearance. Further, she wanted to save her energies for next day's stalk of the handsome soldier. "If I so much as leave the house, Mamma, I know I will simply fall over in a swoon."

Ever hopeful, Sir Marcus pointed out, "You can rest till eight, then come with us for only a few moments. Once you have entered, you can go off to the carriage and return with it, then send it back."

Dulcie had no strength to shake her head more than twice over the details of the prospective agenda.

It was never difficult for Lady Kimball to feel provoked past endurance. "Where on earth have you and Hypatia Innis been on this day, that you return so weary?"

Dulcie's eyes widened briefly in what she hoped her mother wouldn't recognize as alarm. It was a line of questioning that she did not wish to see followed up. With all the strength she could muster she surged to her feet.

"I am weary," Dulcie proclaimed, "and will not allow myself to be tormented in this fashion."

Before either parent could respond, Dulcie had hurried out of the downstairs drawing room.

Lady Kimball was unwilling to be outdone in a display of temperament. Before she could rise in turn, Dulcie was upstairs. Through the opened panel, she and Sir Marcus could hear the girl in her room, hauling a chair over to set it against the door so that she couldn't possibly be interrupted from the hall.

"This," said Lady Kimball, keeping in place only because she recognized the uselessness of an expedition to the upper reaches, "is an infamous outrage."

Sir Marcus shrugged, convinced that the matter was being painted blacker than warranted by necessity, but hardly willing to venture that opinion to his marriage partner.

Lady Kimball chafed at her inability to bludgeon another into performing the parental will. She would have relished bringing Dulcie into Almack's by the scruff of her neck, but the cub was wholly intractable. There must be a way of giving an appearance of normality to a family bereft of a son during the Season. There must be. . . .

"Oh, yes," she said after a pause during which her mind had raced. "Truly I dislike the notion, but I think it is necessary that we accomplish our actual purpose. I think I see one way to do so."

"I'm sure that everything will work out for the best," Sir Marcus agreed pacifically.

"What occurs to me, Marcus, is that it's not necessary to utilize Dulcie's services. We will, as you know, be attending a masked ball and another young female currently resides in the house. With some deft management, I believe that we can surmount the few remaining obstacles."

"*Mirabile dictu,*" her husband murmured feelingly.

Portia had closeted herself all day in this room which Lady Kimball had allotted to her for sleeping and resting. Until several moments ago she had brooded over the iniquity of Jeremy, Lord Newlake, in gaining her affection and then tossing her to another. Crushed though she was, no remedy came to mind. Nor did she relish putting the Kimballs into a wax because she herself was plainly so unhappy. As to her aunt and the likely discussions about Portia's contemptuous behavior toward that puffed-up Lieutenant Turbayne, it was time to face the gorgon and have at the verbal joust in the offing. It wasn't Portia's way to postpone unpleasantness, as a rule.

She was almost glad of the summons to descend as delivered by the ubiquitous Humility. In a bright green day dress and with her dark hair pushed severely back, she joined aunt and uncle in the downstairs drawing room.

"I have given you great latitude in hopes that you would consider your deficiencies and I could then speak to you of them," Lady Kimball began. "Fresh developments, I regret to say, force me to postpone the prolonged and pitiless consideration of your many faults."

"For that much," Portia said honestly and cheekily, "I am grateful."

Lady Kimball was not unaware of the subtler purport of that statement, and Portia fancied she saw Sir Marcus's lips twitch slightly.

"You are to proceed up to your room," Lady Kimball said, spurred to curtness by a sight of her husband's reaction to the girl's feeble jest. "There you will wait for Humility to bring you one of Dulcie's gowns. The fit is almost perfect. Humility will see to it that any needed changes are made and will correct your hair so that you can be coifed sensibly. And you must wear a mask, which we will, of course, provide."

"But to what purpose?" Surely her aunt had no intention of arranging one more meeting for her with Lieutenant Turbayne.

Lady Kimball ignored the question. "We will all be entering with others, so it may be assumed that you are necessarily in our company, as your uncle and I will later aver is true. After a moment, you return to the family carriage, which will take you here, and send it back to wait till your uncle and I are ready to return."

Sir Marcus, listening to the deception as sketched by his wife, felt strongly that it was unnecessary. Had he been a less trusting man it would have occurred to him that as his wife was unable to have her latest *fiat* obeyed by Dulcie, the next-best source of gratification lay in victimizing Dulcie's cousin and new friend. In and of itself, certainly there was little need to force anybody else into this pilgrimage to Almack's.

Portia understood finally that no meeting with Turbayne was planned, but remained puzzled. "I am still not aware of the purpose for these preparations."

Lady Kimball dismissed the interruption with the wave of a hand. Sir Marcus, however, as only to be expected, was kinder.

"You will be of aid to us by doing as your aunt suggests," he said, foregoing complicated explanations and the skepticism they would engender. To mitigate his niece's disappointment, he added, "We will be off to Almack's, the number one haunt of *ton* in the city."

Portia cared little at the moment for visiting the current haunts of *ton*. She had heard Dulcie barricading herself into her room, and supposed that aunt and uncle wanted it to appear that their daughter had joined them at the place of such renown. Portia, like her uncle, gave no thought to her aunt's need to discommode the recalcitrant cousin of her difficult daughter. The suggested ruse did seem to her both needless and overly elaborate, but her participation might later be seen through Dulcies' eyes as a favor.

"I have no stomach for supper, but will go upstairs and dress." Portia smiled at her uncle. "*Pour le sport.*"

The family carriage started off to Almack's at nine-thirty, a tired coachman in front and two nattily uniformed footmen in the rear. Portia's half-formed expectation that the omnipresent maid, Humility, would be among the staff for this purpose, too, was ill-founded, she was glad to observe.

In preparing this foray, Portia had been outfitted with a dazzling green gown, an admirable complement to Dulcie's coloring and almost as good for her own. An absence of faint yellow stripes at the shoulders would have been preferable, to her tastes, but not possible in this dress. Cleavage had once more been hidden at her insistence by a bib. Her hair was parted in the middle and drawn across the forehead, exposing ears rather larger than necessary, but showing attractive flat round plaits behind the head. This design, however, was hidden under an ample leghorn hat. Only the gold mask was unusual for a night's revelry, but not so startling, apparently, in the city.

Lady Kimball, masked like the others, didn't speak till they were passing the horse guards stationed at Piccadilly. "Why are we dawdling?"

"We will arrive quite soon, m'dear," the masked Sir Marcus assured her.

"Before dawn, I trust." Lady Kimball, in black, rustled the dark gray pelisse and set the forget-me-nots in her gray hair to quivering as she tossed her head. "I am in no mood for delay."

"We are approaching St. James's now, and King Street is certainly nearby and Number 26 within walking distance."

Lady Kimball's doubtless snapping rejoinder was lost to Portia as the carriage made a sudden turn. It halted at last, and a footman helped Sir Marcus to alight. While he was adjusting his long brown surtout and touching up the high black velvet collar, Lady Kimball made a magisterial descent and Portia followed with commendable swiftness.

A linkboy lighted the way for them, joining other revelers in their approach to the celebrated joss house of *ton* that was called Almack's. A hum of talk surfaced around them. Portia, for the first time in the higher reaches of society, could hear the talk. As might have been the case in Hove, it was currently centered on a scandal.

"They do say that Mr. Brummell, of all people, has been unable to pay debts and just recently up and ran off to the Continent," a masked gentleman was saying.

"Society will never be the same without the Beau," another remarked.

"I had little patience for his troubles," a third and deeper male voice put in. "He borrowed and knew he wouldn't be able to pay back unless fortune favored him, but fortune did not. He lost a gamble on top of a gamble, and well deserves his portion of gall and wormwood."

The second man shuddered strongly. "I hate to think what would happen if all *my* debts were suddenly called in."

"You, sir, would surely contrive to prosper," the pleasantly deep-voiced man insisted with a laugh.

"By gad, sir, you cover your true opinion like a master of forensic argle-bargle," the second man said admiringly. "I almost regret that you are masked and cannot be recognized."

Portia, unable to keep from listening, had on the contrary instantly recognized that deep and pleasant voice. She nearly called out with anger. Turning to vent her feelings at the deep-voiced man, whose tall build she also picked out immediately in the velvet-trimmed broadcloth draped over an evening suit, she was suddenly touched on an arm by her uncle and knew that she must look away.

She delayed her compliance a moment too long, and almost tripped on a step at the entrance. Soon they were approaching the vestibule to the celebrated assembly rooms. Lady Kimball paused, then turned, and looked pointedly at her niece.

Portia was so concerned with her own feelings, heart pounding furiously, hands closed into small fists, that she didn't instantly observe her aunt's actions. By the time these were plain, Lady Kimball was glaring through the eyeholes of her mask.

At the memorable sight, Portia understood what message her aunt was silently conveying. This was the time for her to depart for the family carriage, to leave the precincts of this hallowed haven of *ton*. Instinctively, Portia nodded and turned to do as she had agreed well in advance. That was when she observed that the deep-voiced rogue had entered by a parallel route and, having divested himself of the cloak, moved on to the vestibule and beyond.

The sight of him from the back reminded Portia keenly how much she ached to tell him that he was a cruelly self-righteous prig who scorned the debts of others but was not above ensnaring the emotions of a young girl and then arranging for her to be offered for at the hands of some coarse stranger. During most of this past minute she had been in the presence of the man she despised, of Jeremy, Lord Newlake.

Her response to having been near him and now finding herself elsewhere was immediate. She rushed ahead in the same direction, conscious only that for her own peace of mind the ever-forthright Portia had to confront that titled rascal.

She did not hear her aunt's voice back of her:

"What is that fool girl doing?" Lady Kimball asked the world in shrill tones.

It was a pointless question, for Sir Marcus's wife must have known perfectly well that her niece was charging into the vestibule and aiming herself like one of the Duke of Wellington's roaring cannons at the inner bastions of placid and unruffled society.

CHAPTER 11

Portia had not reckoned on the difficulty of maintaining a constant pitch of anger in a place, bordered by potted palms, where others were taking their ease or engaged in banter, or eating and drinking from tables off to one side. A quadrille had been concluded, and several young fops were concernedly studying the establishment's quadrille *carte d'instruction,* all looking as if they'd heard that language could be printed but had never previously encountered specimens of the craft. The clearest difference between members of this assemblage and those at Colonel Duggin's *déclassé* party of last night was that the celebrants before her now were quieter and more decorous, as if not wanting to admit that they were finding pleasure in this occasion. If such a distinction alone separated the pinks of *ton* from the whites and grays of other groups, very little was being adduced to speak the praises of good society.

It was when this thought penetrated to Portia's intelligence that she knew her anger might be ebbing. To give it fresh life, she scanned the room until noting that Jeremy Newlake was still deeply absorbed in conversation with the men to whom he had been speaking a while before. It seemed that no one else existed for him at the moment in this most discreet and mannerly of possible worlds.

A familiar voice, of the subspecies female this time, caused her to look away. Lady Kimball was speaking urgently to her husband in words that couldn't be distinguished from so far away. No doubt the elder couple had entered and given three tickets to the factotum at the door, not wanting a scandal in regard to a family connection. The elders must also have been aware that the factotum had only coped with a previous rush of entrants by not halting Portia in her tracks as she hurtled herself past the pearly gates, so to speak.

Glancing across the room, the miscreant had no doubt that Sir Marcus was being informed that he must be the one to persuade Portia to leave. Probably that course was urged upon him because a male would be a more impressive source of authority to any young girl and, further, she seemed to favor her uncle in dealings with the couple. Sir Marcus nodded, then swallowed, turned, and started his walk with the object of joining her. His undoubted reluctance to attempt this designated objective made that walk slower than would have been the case otherwise.

Portia, determined not to submit before she had spoken her bitterness to Newlake, turned in his direction to glower. Jeremy Newlake, resplendent in gleaming short boots, buckled breeches, a dark coat, a rigid collar and mercilessly starched cravat, felt the glare and swung his glass in her direction. Without looking away from her, the peer spoke quietly to those men gathered around him, making a gesture of apology with one hand. Then he started over to her.

This was a development which Portia hadn't expected, although at an assembly to which three men had properly been vouchered for every unmarried female similarly honored, it was not, on further consideration, unlikely. Should he ask a dance, as seemed possible, her uncle would not be able to remonstrate with her until she had dealt with this polished rascal. At the moment, he was advancing upon her from one direction and her uncle from the opposite.

As always, fortune favored the bold. Jeremy Newlake reached Portia first, then allowed himself to sound puzzled; it was impossible to see what his features behind a dark and shiny mask may have been expressing.

"I am searching for your escort, of whom I might ask permission for a dance."

She realized that her own mask had made it impossible in turn for him to sense her emotions. He must have felt that he was tactfully accepting a silent invitation. The sound of that thrillingly deep voice, speaking words addressed to her, moved Portia despite the ruling of her mind.

"Do you wish to sport a toe with my aunt?" she asked coolly, softening her bitterness by adopting a tone of mild sarcasm. "That would be suitable but difficult for a lively tune."

"I only hope to gain permission for a dance with you and then return you to her protection," he explained patiently, as if she didn't know. He declined to be incited by this condescending tone, not even questioning its suitability from a maiden who had almost certainly wanted his advances. He was showing a level of patience to which Portia felt she could never aspire.

Sir Marcus, less than six feet off, paused to observe the outcome of this colloquy, not wanting to draw the man's ire at an interruption. Portia knew that if she reproached Jeremy bitterly at this point, Sir Marcus would interfere on the young peer's behalf even if he hadn't recognized the black sheep of the Newlake clan.

"Sir, I will accept responsibility and permit myself to dance with you."

"I am honored."

Portia had anticipated that some form of quadrille would be struck up by the musicians, who were playing from behind a group of palms, a vantage from which neither they nor the audience would be visible to the other. In this way, during a Lancer, for instance, she would not be dancing with him at every moment, and certainly it would be simplicity itself to avoid even his lightest touch.

Unfortunately it was a waltz which was struck up, that devil's tool as introduced by Princess de Lieven at the Russian embassy before sweeping the city and its environs as thoroughly as the Great Fire of 1666. As a result of its being known in Sussex, Portia was richly knowledgeable in the perils of this justly celebrated *Waltzentanz*.

He touched her at the back, then took her hand in his. Expecting to loathe that tactile experience and be correspondingly unable to pretend to even an outward show of politeness, she felt instead that her heart missed a beat because of this pleasure. Being moved in such a way by her tormentor was both horrid and inexplicably delightful.

For the next moments, all breath was nearly swept out of her body as he moved across the floor with her. He showed grace and balance, to say nothing of great thoughtfulness to a partner. These attributes she had never before encountered so generously on an assembly floor. A quick look at other London males nearby showed that they were not universally so accommodating. That look also showed Sir Marcus, standing with arms akimbo as he listened to his wife rating him for not having dragooned Portia—although Lady Kimball must have been doing it quietly enough so as not to draw unseemly attention from revelers.

Portia told herself that she was too much out of breath to speak her fury to this peer, however keenly she wanted to do so.

"Despite the mask," he suddenly said, with a cheery demeanor that she found odious, "I was able to identify you at first sight."

She felt certain he was being complimentary, employing the discretion for which he was famous in Parliament and loathed by Portia.

"But you fear to speak my name," she said, getting out the words in spite of the exertion. She was determined to trap him in this small lie, at least, and use it as a springboard for the accusations she would make before the conclusion of this whirl.

But he asked, "Do you think that I don't know Portia Galton with a mask as well as without?"

Despite the lack of ammunition, even a small amount, she rallied her forces to strike a devastating blow elsewhere.

"And your conscience doesn't bother you?"

Because she was nearly out of breath, it became impossible to speak with the intensity that she favored in quarrels. As a result, he may have assumed that she was being frisky.

"My conscience? Why should it offer me the least worry?"

Her silence, corresponding to a pause between tunes, must have been so deliberate that he realized the serious nature of this conversation to her sensibilities.

"'Pon my word, I don't know the answer," he said, looking directly into her eyes. "You are a most forthright person" (did she sense a certain envy from that distinguished Parliamentarian?) "and I feel sure that you will inform me."

The original offense had been magnified by those words, it seemed to the anguished Portia. Having betrayed another, a subsequent denial of the least wrong was simply monstrous.

She took action without giving it any thought in advance. Drawing back from the peer, she raised a palm.

"Here is something that will encourage you to think about it," she said angrily, and slapped him full across a cheek.

She was aware of a hubbub of conversation as she ran away blindly, tears stinging her eyes. Jeremy Newlake's voice rose clearly, calling to her past the circle of well-wishers that had formed around him. She ran to the entrance and heard his voice yet again, but this time as a murmur addressed to others, and then there was a chuckle from a few throats. He had passed off the entire scalding incident with some pleasantry, avoiding further questions and making light of another human's deep distress.

Portia ran out to the Kimball berline at long last and, sobbing bitterly, was taken back to Jermyn Street.

CHAPTER 12

The masked friends who had clustered around to succor
Jeremy in his moment of need were soon assured of his composure, largely because of the delicate wit he showed. These
dispersed accordingly, to resume their own concerns. Jeremy,
however, leaving the dance floor, was secretly appalled. He
had previously made it clear that he was taken with Portia
Galton, and Miss Galton had welcomed his burgeoning interest. But now she had chosen to display anger at him, and he
had to learn what impulse had spurred her on.

His best hope of accomplishing this goal with dispatch was
to find Dulcie in the crowd and subject her to vigorous questioning. He would have recognized his childhood friend no
matter how many masks she chose to wear. A few minutes of
searching were enough to convince him, however, that she
was not to be found here.

Possibly Sir Marcus or Lady Kimball would proffer assistance, but Jeremy was not so well acquainted with those an-
cients as to recognize either in a masked group. He could understand as well why neither Kimball came to him, as they
must have hoped that Portia had somehow escaped identifica-
tion.

For once, Jeremy was lacking in perseverance. Otherwise
he would have waited till those revellers who decided to un-
mask finally did so. To his way of thinking, though, the conun-
drum had to be resolved as soon as humanly possible.

Searching his mind for a possible cause of the difficulty, he
recollected that it was he who had put Lieutenant Ivor Tur-

bayne of the Seventh Foot in contact with the family. That officer was desirous of marrying for a splendid dowry, and Sir Marcus had pointed out with becoming *sangfroid* that for an unmarried young female, time passed far too speedily.

It had taken Jeremy aback not to receive any communication from Sir Marcus as to the success of this military maneuver, so to speak, in providing a happy future for Dulcie. That particular lack, now recollected, made him wonder if Turbayne had in some fashion demeaned Dulcie, and her cousin had responded vigorously in consequence. It seemed unlikely, considering that the lieutenant's self-assurance would enthrall the likes of his childhood friend, but the possibility deserved a thorough investigation.

So absorbed was he by the problem that while retrieving his cloak he was not distracted even briefly by a memorable witticism. He happened to overhear George Dawson-Damer, not generally renowed for verbal acuity, skeptically discussing the suicide attempt of a mutual friend.

"I cannot believe that a man like Tubby, who relishes the pleasures of the table, would seriously care to curtail his own existence," Dawson-Damer said spiritedly. "He might prove such an intent to himself, however, by purposely falling on his butter-knife."

Despite this venture into the higher realms of philosophy, Jeremy remained in a pensive mood as he swept out to the street and his waiting curricle. He was in no mood to drive for pleasure, even if he hadn't expected to imbibe a touch more than necessary and had therefore brought a coachman with two footmen to convoy him. The former was directed to drive to Gentleman Jackson's Boxing Saloon, on Bond Street.

It was in this establishment that he could very possibly find the answer at a gratifying speed. Here an Army officer was likely to be found of a night if he hadn't chosen to engage himself in an affair of the heart or seek the favors of a demirep. Should Turbayne himself not be among those present, some fellow officer from the Seventh Foot would surely inform Jeremy of the outcome to last night's attempt to begin the quest for financial happiness by way of female companionship.

In the saloon itself, which was to boxing what Almack's was to sport of another hue, an exhibition was in progress. John Jackson, the Gentleman himself, was sporting with one of the Fancy, a younger connection of the Second Baron Muskerry, if Jeremy wasn't mistaken. Jackson was most assuredly carrying the young man along. He boxed discreetly, as befit the pugilist who had taught the manly art of fisticuffs to such of the gentry as Lord Byron and who hobnobbed pleasurably with others. He had not always been so perfectly behaved in the ring, having won the championship back in '95 from the Jew Mendoza by gripping his opponent's long hair with one hand and then clubbing him with the other.

Not only were the gentry welcome, but so were Army and Navy officers, as has been said, for they could be considered fighters of another stripe. The premises fairly bristled with Army elite at the moment.

Good eyesight alone was required to discover the astonishingly handsome Turbayne. He was in a corner and cheering for Jackson to demolish the blood who was facing him. Jeremy wasn't altogether surprised by the revelation of Turbayne's true feelings toward the gentry.

At the courteous gesture that drew his attention, an abashed Turbayne joined him where the noise wasn't so pervasive.

"I only waked up a little ago, having been asleep through the day as is my custom when on leave," Turbayne began hastily, imparting a revelation that Dulcie alone would have been interested to hear. It would have clarified for her why she hadn't observed that doughty officer in Hyde Park or by the premises of his hotel. "Not being in total command of myself for that reason, I cheered a mite hastily and injudiciously, I fear."

Jeremy accepted the apology with a shrug, diplomatically overlooking the evidence of Turbayne's perfectly natural enmity toward those of greater position or wealth. The officer's feelings on this point were of little interest.

Turbayne allowed himself to fall silent, certain that his feeble fiction had impelled belief. It indicated much about the officer's character if he was convinced that a statement spoken doggedly by him would promptly gain acceptance.

Jeremy had known Turbayne along with some other officers of the Seventh Foot, but his mind had rested on Ivor immediately when a respectable if not inspired candidate for marriage with Dulcie Kimball had been quickly needed. There was a simple reason for this. In the course of his life, Jeremy had become used to seeing farmers who, instead of being gaunt after so much hard work, were apple-cheeked and portly. Nor was it unusual to encounter curates who looked as if they could have entered the squared circle with Jackson or Mendoza or any of their ilk. But Ivor Turbayne was exactly as he appeared, a ramrod-straight, impeccably turned-out officer of the Crown; and one would have guessed his calling if he had been found in rags. An officer's services as a husband had been requested, so the first who had come to mind was an officer in every outward way.

Jeremy, concentrating on the matter of moment, asked, "Did this meeting last night go well?"

"Splendidly," the officer said. "All on pitch, so to say."

Inevitably, his dogged certainty forced Jeremy to pursue further inquiries.

"Tell me what happened."

Turbayne threw his handsome head back, like a bay horse refusing the bit. "As I say, it was all according to plan. However, there was a minor setback."

Jeremy was not surprised, and sought even further clarification. "May I now ask in detail what went wrong?"

"I hope, sir, that you will do so." In the tactful pause, it occurred to the Pride of the Seventh Foot that the question had indeed been put. "It was the girl herself, sir, who posed the minor difficulty. A ninnyhammer with less in the way of good manners I have never encountered in my life."

Jeremy felt himself pulled up short. Having known Dulcie for so many years, it wouldn't have occurred to him for a moment to consider that she was lacking in *politesse* as a rule, any more than he was himself.

"And you did nothing to give offense to a delicately nurtured young woman?"

"Certainly not, sir. I told her that I would dance the next quadrille with her, and was subjected to some—ah, as I say, difficulty."

This last statement Jeremy put down to military hyperbole of the sort that proclaimed the trembling of a leaf to be the start of a planned insurrection. Dulcie would have snubbed the man so politely he would never have known what took place.

"Mind you," Turbayne added reflectively, "I confess that I would prefer the other girl, who is amiable and lovely, and looks as if she would appreciate the strong leadership which is necessary in marriage, as I have been given to understand."

Jeremy was now entirely at sea. The officer was apparently describing Dulcie as a tartar and Portia as mild and biddable. He didn't consider that any of Turbayne's characterizations was weighted down with so much as a scintilla of accuracy.

"Let me have a little added information, for I am perplexed," Jeremy said. "The girl with whom you wished to dance—she was a light-haired young lady, is that not true?"

"No, sir. The light-haired young lady is the one who was very sweet."

Jeremy, taking a long breath, restrained his temper with a force that would have done credit to the late William Pitt debating with Mr. Fox as to the procedure by which the Prince of Wales could be appointed to the Regency.

"You apparently made a slight error," he informed the Pride of the Seventh Foot. "Instead of honoring Miss Kimball, you chose to work your wiles on Miss Portia Galton. She is a niece of the elder Kimballs, and does not take kindly to such attempts to ingratiate oneself as you describe. In other words, you approached the wrong girl."

Ivor Turbayne shook his head firmly. "Begging your pardon, sir, but I must disagree."

"Are you telling me, Lieutenant, that I don't know one girl from the other?"

"I am only insisting, sir, that I did not go to the wrong girl."

"But you admit by the descriptions that you sought out Miss Galton for the dance."

"Exactly."

Jeremy was not bereft of common sense. "Miss Galton was the *right* girl?"

"Yes. Sir Marcus met me at the rout last night and pointed her out to me in advance, the dark-haired one, the niece, for whom it had been intended that I offer."

The words could hardly have been more simple, yet Jeremy felt as if he had sustained a punch in the solar plexus from John Jackson himself. It was easy to understand now that Portia, convinced of Jeremy Newlake's genuine and strong interest in her, had been incensed to be told by the Pride of the Seventh Foot that it was Lord Newlake who had helped bring them together—and certainly the likes of Turbayne would seek to make his *bona fides* absolutely impeccable.

It dazed Jeremy even more, though this hardly seemed possible, that he should have been the one to suggest another husband for that girl in whom he himself had become so keenly interested. True, he hadn't at that time known enough to connect Portia with the Kimballs, so that the error was as natural as it remained astonishing.

A few carefully chosen words would suffice to thank Turbayne for telling him all, and send the officer back to observe the outcome of those fisticuffs taking place in the arena. Turbayne impeded Jeremy's stratagem by clearing his throat forcefully, a clear indication that he wished to offer a coda to the solo he had just performed.

"Please understand," Turbayne added, "that if I still have the approval of Sir Marcus and his lady I remain prepared, as before, to offer for the girl. I have written to Sir Marcus and Lady Kimball to say so."

Ivor Turbayne was most likely unwilling to appear fazed by any difficulty however crucial. It was an attitude that his military training had inculcated more deeply in what must already have been fertile ground, or so Jeremy felt convinced.

"You shouldn't pursue it further," Jeremy said quickly but evenly. "The current condition of your relationship with Miss Galton seems an unlikely augury for years of connubial happiness."

"In the Army, sir, I would spend much time away from home," the officer pointed out virtuously. "Under those terms, a marriage even to her could be tolerable."

"Think of the unhappiness when you two had to see each other."

"For a man of my station, sir, without true position or any wealth to speak of, the prospect of a dowry is sufficiently inviting to make up for much in the way of possible tribulation."

The point would not have been easy to dispute. Confronted by the likelihood of Turbayne's winning the agreement of uncle and aunt, who almost certainly wanted to marry Portia into a rank below *ton* so as not to invite comparisons that could be of no advantage to Dulcie, Jeremy perceived that action must be taken. The calamity of his unintentional *gaffe* had to be redressed as soon as possible. Once again he must be the recipient of Portia Galton's good feelings. Then he would be able to deal with the Kimballs from a vantage of strength.

How this ambitious program was to be accomplished, however, he did not immediately know.

CHAPTER 13

Thursday morning at the Kimball *ménage* began with one of those characteristic spans of inactivity which is the inalienable privilege of the upper class and its acolytes. Sir Marcus took breakfast while wearing an embroidered dressing gown and contemplated his thick steaming chocolate as he pored meditatively over a copy of the *Morning Post*.

The calm was soothing, as Beatrice was not yet awake to tell him in detail how greatly she was distressed because of the previous night's unsuitable behavior by Portia at Almack's. After the couple had unmasked at the assembly, they had pretended to others that they had recognized no one connected with the disconcerting incident. So busily were they establishing their ignorance or that of any family connection that they had almost forgotten to tell of Lionel's leaving home and to claim that their son had acted with freely given parental approval.

Upon their late arrival back at Jermyn Street, Lady Kimball had wanted nothing more than to ascend to her husband's niece Portia's room and give her the sharp end of a cruel tongue. No matter if it was now proved beyond cavil that Portia would not be appealing to Jeremy Newlake, an opportunity for criticism had been offered and she felt that it must be taken.

Sir Marcus ventured to point out that such a *brouhaha* as indicated might disturb neighbors. Lady Kimball was forced to concede that point but was determined to speak with pitiless sharpness in the morning. One or two difficult hours loomed for Sir Marcus and his niece.

Sir Marcus hoped that there would be no mention of last night's galamatias in the gossipy newspaper before him. In this he was destined for disappointment. The *Post* reported that incident without giving names. Sir Marcus knew that Jeremy was too much the gentleman ever to speak against a relative of Dulcie's, but felt annoyed by this example of the gossip's art and craft.

The day's letters offered a new and unexpected development. There was a screed from Lieutenant Turbayne in which that worthy aggrievedly proclaimed his continued willingness to offer for Portia despite her behavior at Colonel Duggin's rout. Sir Marcus was grateful, if only because Beatrice would be calmed by the knowledge that not all had been lost in the matter of settling Portia as soon as humanly possible.

Beatrice, when she joined Sir Marcus for a late breakfast of strong tea and scones, looked as if she had slept soundly and was anticipating the battle with Portia. Upon perusing the letter, which Sir Marcus had handed over, she nodded determinedly.

"Something more to take up with her," Beatrice averred, with a glint in her eye that resembled that of a tiger stalking its prey.

Sir Marcus carefully interposed an objection. "Do you think that after having met the lieutenant she will want to marry him?"

"She must do so if we have to bludgeon her into it."

"The bludgeon hasn't been a very successful weapon against Portia up to this date."

"It hasn't been tried with sufficient severity." Lady Kimball demolished a scone as if she were a tiger snapping the spine of its prey. "Portia must be made so unhappy every time she sees us that she will long to escape. Very quickly it will be borne in upon her that marriage is the way to accomplish this desired end."

It was a fiercely practical suggestion, the sort that Sir Marcus would have expected from a helpmate involved with protecting her own daughter at the expense of another. But the knight cringed inwardly at the prospect of so many head-to-head encounters as his wife envisaged.

"I think I will be spending many mealtimes from now on at my clubs."

Beatrice nodded, understanding his manly reticence and nothing loath to accept a duty which she did not find at all onerous. Nevertheless, she couldn't help making a pronouncement about her husband's disinclination to be of help.

"All males are cowards when it comes to the truly important duties in life," said the surviving daughter of Lucretia Armadale with utter conviction.

Sir Marcus did not discuss the point. He was busily seeking out clothes for an early-morning trip. It hardly mattered that his clubs were to be shut for a while longer. He would alight somewhere and return only after supper.

Portia, as it happened, was not averse to picking up the gauntlet in any battle that might ensue. If conflict was necessary she would participate, having prepared by taking revenge upon Jeremy Newlake. She felt as if she were not an instrument to be buffeted, but could herself take arms against a sea of troubles, in the words of some minstrel whose name escaped her.

The late breakfast proved, all the same, to be a difficult time. Lady Kimball, having previously eaten, participated only by arguing. Where her aunt thrust, Portia parried. Lady Kimball, becoming more irritated and unable to bring up any point she had not already put forth, kept making the same thrusts. Portia, eating determinedly, responded with the same parries.

Dulcie appeared last, anticipating an argument between Mamma and herself over her refusal to join the family at Almack's. That particular dispute did not materialize, as Mamma was kept too busy enumerating the fancied iniquities of her cousin. It was the sort of battering to which Dulcie had often succumbed, and she found it instructive that Portia argued in return, if with the respect due an elder. Portia even managed to take a full breakfast with added cups of tea.

It was Lady Kimball who retired from the lists for the moment. Not that she was exhausted, but a number of letters had to be written and could not be further postponed. The battle was going to be resumed at another time and place of her choice, probably when she next saw Portia. On the strength of much experience, Lady Kimball remained sublimely confident of her ability to wear the girl down.

Portia and her cousin repaired to the upper drawing room, where Portia recounted the incident of her last night's outburst at "the assembly place," as she called Almack's.

Dulcie's face didn't show if she was tempted to laughter at the image of so many celebrants disturbed. As might have been expected, she remained entirely sympathetic.

"Jemmy Newlake received nothing more than he richly deserved," she insisted stoutly, turning from the spinet which she had tentatively approached in order to exercise her greatest social accomplishment.

Rather than coolly thanking her cousin, Portia embraced her. Dulcie was unused to such a show from anybody, but returned the embrace with unfeigned enthusiasm.

"I will certainly tell Jemmy Newlake what I think of him," she insisted afterward, tossing her head angrily on Portia's behalf. "How dared he to use you the way he did!"

Portia doubted if being slanged by Dulcie would go far to convince Jeremy Newlake about the error of his ways, but kept that uncertainty to herself.

"My life would have been a horror if Jemmy had offered for me, I can see that now," Dulcie continued warmly.

She was prepared to embroider this theme further, but sunlight through the north window suddenly reached her face and she looked away with some embarrassment.

Portia understood what was in her cousin's mind. "It is now the beginning of afternoon and time for you to leave."

Dulcie nodded, seeing no necessity to say that she would soon be off to Hyde Park in hopes of seeing and then talking with Ivor Turbayne. Should the officer not appear with others in pursuit of converse with young ladies, she intended, as before, to proceed to the front of Stephen's Hotel and wait for him to make an appearance.

"I know that you don't like Ivor, but I feel sure that an upright officer like him will be the proper man for me to marry. True, we have not so much as spoken to one another, not yet, but we did exchange what I might call smoldering glances, so I think he is interested too."

Portia smiled, accepting once again the knowledge that Dulcie's tastes and inclinations in some areas were different from hers. Indeed Portia had assimilated this intelligence when Dulcie first spoke about her burgeoning passion, if such it could be considered.

"Good luck," she said sincerely, and recalled Dulcie's kindness in conferring an affectionate honorific on her, even though it had subsequently been discarded in the bustle of everyday life. "Good luck, sister."

Dulcie remembered too, and flushed happily. "What you should say is 'good hunting,'" she responded with a laugh and added in turn, "sister."

In hopes of avoiding Lady Kimball's company, Portia resorted to the perusal of a five-shilling guidebook to London, but did it only lackadaisically. She found herself remembering Jeremy Newlake and how well they had fit together on the assembly floor, each being the correct height for the other. She gasped at an onrush of belated modesty and returned her eyes to a description of Westminster Hall in Parliament as embellished with a listing of those historical figures who had been condemned to death in that chamber. Because Jeremy Newlake sat in the Lords, she suddenly felt concerned for his neck, then realized that no such harm would befall him in these enlightened times. She ended her inspection of the guidebook by hurling it onto a pseudo-oriental chair.

Lady Kimball didn't seek her out, but only because of being occupied with social visitors who had arrived in hopes of enjoying the inestimable boon of her company. Luckily, too, Portia was not asked to descend and meet those doubtless exalted personages. It would have been more than she was able to tolerate.

Sir Marcus wisely shunned supper, which offered moments of discomfort for those who participated. Dulcie had again been disappointed in her quest for the elusive Ivor, but on this occasion managed to eat, even if sadly. Portia, once again berated by her aunt, answered in the same words as before. She knew no others to utilize, not realizing that the repetition was enough to further incense Lady Kimball.

At the conclusion of supper Lady Kimball distracted herself from hostilities. "Portia, you will accompany your cousin and myself to the Theatre Royal in Drury Lane this night."

No doubt the occasion offered more opportunities for other acrid if *sub rosa* complaints against this erring, in her view, niece. Portia, whose patience for mummers involved with pretense was little greater than her aversion to opera, didn't look forward to the occasion, for two separate and distinct reasons rather than the expected single cause.

Dulcie, however, became almost enthusiastic when the two girls returned to her room.

"Ivor might be in the audience," she explained eagerly before Portia could inquire the reason for this sudden access of vitality after a wearying day. "I could converse with him if only for a few moments and we would be clear beyond question about one another's feelings."

The prospect of Portia accordingly being left alone with Lady Kimball, if only for a few moments, was far from pleasant. She offered no adverse comment, however. Spending a little time in greater propinquity with a gorgon was the very least she could do in aid of the cousin who made life in *le monde* even remotely tolerable.

Dulcie loaned her a white silk gown, a merino pelisse, and a discreet hat so that she wouldn't put Lady Kimball to shame by not being dressed to the crack of fashion. Portia insisted, however, on wearing her own French silk stockings and so-called Moroccan leather shoes. In this array, and white-gloved to the elbows, she joined the others, *sans* the prudent Sir Marcus, who remained immured at White's Club despite this festive occasion.

Lady Kimball chafed in silence, unable to criticize Portia because of the footmen in hearing distance. Dulcie spoke instead, letting Portia know of the event she had read about and which they would soon be witnessing on the Drury Lane stage. It seemed that one of the multifarious family of Kembles, actors nearly all of them, would favor a paying audience with his current interpretation of the title role in *The Life and Death of King Richard the Second*. The knowledge of this world-shattering circumstance was accepted by Portia with a magnificent display of equanimity.

The rituals of arriving and taking their places in a stuffy box were completed. An actor appeared on stage to represent that departed monarch whose achievements were to be celebrated on this night. He was the loudest-voiced in a group of *flâneurs* who posed as other notabilities, here a Lancaster, there a York, a panoply of Berkeleys and Surreys and Norfolks, with a Northumberland added. Portia's state of indifference altered to one of near torpor.

The actor who impersonated Richard was loudly contemplating a visit to the deathbed of the Duke of Lancaster when the curtain was lowered for a blessed *entr'acte*. Lady Kimball, having been unable to rate Portia since their arrival because the play had begun just after they were seated, suddenly leaned over to remonstrate quietly with her for not having been polite to "dear Lieutenant Turbayne" when the two had met. Portia responded precisely as she had done in the past, and fled before making some remark to an elder that would be unforgivable.

She found herself in a long hall. Theatergoers strode back and forth or chatted in groups about the performance but not the content of the play. Some officers were to be seen. Lieutenant Turbayne, however, wasn't among them. Had the opportunity offered, she would certainly have informed that popinjay about Dulcie's wanting to speak with him.

The crowd was becoming thinner in numbers, a certain signal that the refined torture of watching thespians was shortly to resume. Portia was about to follow the audience's example, however reluctantly, and go back to the arms of culture, as well as, in her case, the voice and presence of Lady Kimball, when she heard a soft and deep masculine voice behind her.

"I hoped I would find you at this event which has captured so many of London's elect," said Jeremy Newlake.

CHAPTER 14

Portia's heart fluttered as she whirled around, and then she told herself that she remained furious with this deceiver. All the same, she could not bring herself to leave his presence. Perhaps she stayed because of a pronounced unwillingness to observe the flummery within this establishment, or so she told herself. A suspicion had come to her, though, that she was at the moment physically unable to move.

"I had to be at the Lords all day because of a heated discussion in which the services of a mediator were urgently needed." With that apology, as he conceived it, Jeremy looked even further ill at ease despite being attired in the proper dark wear for evening. He wished desperately that he could have worked off a little of the tension in him by driving a coach for sport, as he often did when in this condition. "Otherwise I would have come out to Jermyn Street, for I feel it necessary that we speak before anything else can be done."

It was on the tip of Portia's tongue to mock-commiserate with him for last night's happening at Almack's, but she had small capacity to fence with words.

Instead she asked bitterly, "Have you planned upon offering me to yet another member of the armed force? A naval officer this time, perhaps?"

"I can explain what happened."

"What you can surely do is to invent reasons, such as that I dreamed you ingratiated yourself with me and then offered me to some other male."

"An understandable error took place, Portia, and I want you to know just how it came to be."

"You can lie and circumvent facts with the best of them, being in the Lords as you are."

He was about to put in smilingly that she spoke those last words like an aggrieved ratepayer. But she was totally serious, and it behooved him to honor her by responding similarly.

"Will I be permitted to explain?"

"I see no necessity for that, Lord Newlake."

She did not walk off, however, still feeling that she must have been too indignant to do anything but stand glowering at him. Further keeping her in place were the words filtering through from the stage, where the actors posing as King Richard and John of Gaunt were making loud speeches in turn, and she shuddered strongly at the prospect of understanding every word.

Jeremy observed only that she hadn't yet moved, and spoke quickly. "Your uncle approached me before I knew you were part of his family. He asked me in a roundabout fashion to discover a groom for a young lady and stated that a soldier would be suitable, an officer. I know that there is an Army precedent in Sir Marcus's immediate family, thanks to the late heroic Colonel Alisdair Kimball and I assumed it had been decided to marry off Dulcie with somewhat unseemly haste."

There was a plausible air to this statement, understandably falling far short of the *mea culpa* she had at first felt he ought to be making. Her impulse was to keep him on tenterhooks by saying that she would consider this explanation, which she already believed, then return to the box with Dulcie and Lady Kimball as duty required. She was incapable of even this slight dissimulation, and didn't doubt that her features showed it.

Encouraged by her response, he committed himself further.

"Now that I have your approval of my course until this point, I plan to request a visit with your uncle at Jermyn Street tomorrow evening, when he will surely be available. There I can speak with him in private and let you know very quickly if the response is favorable. Although he would have preferred a different class of suitor in your case, I expect I can persuade him and Lady Kimball as well to agree with our plans. I am known as a most persuasive man, as I may tell you with a total lack of modesty."

"And you will offer for m—?" She couldn't get out all the words, for once. Portia, who had always prided herself on speaking directly, was now hardly able to speak at all.

Jeremy, that man of legendary discretion, was impelled by the sight of her radiant features to throw his last reserve to the winds. "I have loved you from the moment we met at Jermyn Street, and I feel sure that you know it."

She began to nod, but was unable to complete that gesture. Without even a look to reassure himself that no one else was in sight, he took her in his arms and lowered his lips to hers. The kiss was firm but all too brief.

There was a moment of awed silence between them as he released her. Portia felt quite dizzy, and would have experienced the gravest difficulty in speaking.

"It is best to go our separate ways now," Jeremy said, having impelled himself to think ahead. "If your aunt happens to discover us together out here and before I am prepared to deal with her and Marcus, explanations might be awkward even for me."

Perfectly true, yet she was unable to make a move away from him.

Jeremy swallowed twice and said, "We will see each other again tomorrow evening, and from that point all is going to be well."

She remained rooted in place.

Jeremy managed to take a step back and then turn. He was

leaving the Drury Lane, convinced that it would have been overpoweringly difficult for him to sit through the performance apart from her.

With some feat of control which Portia found stunning by its precision, he accomplished the task of departing from this hallway without looking around at her. Anyone who blundered into this area would have seemed to be observing a dapper *homme du monde* escaping from the presence of a love-sick young girl.

Portia could not feel the carpeting under the Moroccan leather shoes as she returned slowly to the playing area of the Drury Lane. Her only regret was that the meeting seemed all too short, mostly because she was unable to fence with words and thereby keep him in attendance upon her for a longer time. She had never before regretted her inability to behave in any but a straightforward manner. Indirection was not a trait that she found admirable in misses or gentlemen, but there was something to be said in its favor.

As she reached the family's box, the mummer who was depicting the Earl of Salisbury had started braying at another who was enacting the role of a captain. To Portia's wandering wits it all seemed pleasant now, giving her a chance to consider the passage that had taken place between her and Jeremy, to remember each word and see in her mind the sincerity of various expressions on his face and then joyfully to recollect the brief closeness between them and their passionate kiss.

Lady Kimball, glancing sourly over to her niece, observed that Portia looked distinctively attractive. The flush of cheeks was striking, as were the lips attractively thinned in an unprovoked smile.

Lady Kimball realized once more that a man could become enraptured by the charms of a young maid looking so lovely, and marry beneath him despite all common sense. A vis-

count, a lord, a duke, an earl, any of these males could turn
into a devoted suitor of Portia, disgracing Dulcie forever in
the eyes of society as a result. Lady Kimball did not seriously
consider that a knight or baronet would act on such an afflic-
tion even if one or both fell prey to it, such men being concerned with improving their position to the exclusion of all
else.

Some action must be taken, she decided, even more quickly
than previously planned. The contents of Ivor Turbayne's recent missive to her husband came to mind immediately, and
as she settled back to return her eyes to the play she was
composing a personal answer to that acquisitive officer.

CHAPTER 15

Portia was determined to stay in her room all day and look out the window to see if Jeremy came earlier than expected. She realized the pointlessness of this activity after the first hour, but declined to leave her room and let her presence be abrasive to Lady Kimball before her aunt's approval of the prospective union with Jeremy would be needed. She vainly attempted to immerse herself once more in the five-shilling guidebook to London that she had previously acquired.

Dulcie came to see her, disappointed because Turbayne had proved invisible at the theater. Portia, compelling herself to pay attention to her cousin's worries, sympathized and refrained from saying that she fancied Turbayne's interests as running to coarser pursuits. She was herself no great friend of the lieutenant's, but in this matter blamed him not at all.

It took greater control to keep from talking of Jeremy. She felt that Dulcie was exclusively preoccupied with confirming the strength of Turbayne's feelings toward her. Dulcie left for her afternoon trip to park and hotel front, thinking in turn that Portia seemed, for once, somewhat *distrait*.

As for Lady Kimball, she had attired herself in a white muslin day dress and sent the ever-available Humility on a morning mission to Stephen's Hotel. There the maid had delivered a letter at the clerk's desk and returned home. Sir Marcus had made a hasty exit but not before promising to return by five for the *pourparlers* with their guest, Jemmy Newlake.

The house was hers, except for Portia, who might appear

unexpectedly. Lady Kimball instructed Humility to station herself at the base of the stairs in the afternoon and inform her mistress if Portia descended unexpectedly. With that much done, she needed only to proceed to the drawing room and await the guest whose presence she wanted none to perceive.

Daltrey, the gray-haired butler, announced Lieutenant Turbayne's arrival and nimbly stepped aside. The lieutenant, a sight to behold in his parade uniform of scarlet coat with white crossbelt and white duck trousers, had already given the butler his cloak and bearskin shako with its black-and-red plume. Courteously, too, he had refrained from wearing that saber in its gold scabbard which would have completed his rig.

"I came in response to your letter," he began, striding forward and avoiding the furniture that had been meticulously placed. Dulcie would have been stunned to see the handsome officer at Jermyn Street, but not best pleased to observe that he was sleepy after a long though contenting night. "You wrote that we would discuss something that is very much to my advantage."

"As indeed we will."

At her gesture, Turbayne accepted the stiff chair that was indicated. He crossed his legs. Wincing, Lady Kimball showed how much she abhorred that informality. The Pride of the Seventh promptly uncrossed them. That little by-play was instructive, inasmuch as it convinced Lady Kimball that the man could be worn down by a woman's guiles.

"It is to your advantage, Lieutenant Turbayne, to marry my niece."

"True, but the matter has, for obvious reasons of which you must be aware, become far more distasteful for me. Since writing to Sir Marcus I have conned on it, and am not sure that I would wish to make the effort of taming such a hellion."

Lady Kimball was not bluffed by these protestations. Had he not been amenable, he would never have agreed to closet himself with her. Until this point, her directness would almost have gained Portia's reluctant approval. Now it was time for subtlety, for the indirect manipulation of another, which had become the greatest outlet for Lady Kimball's energies since her own marriage these many years past.

"Surely, Lieutenant Turbayne, you do not admit defeat at the hands of a female."

"There has been no defeat," the officer insisted firmly. "If I wanted to, in spite of her female twaddle, I would instruct Miss Galton that the wedding must be performed."

He would never accept, apparently, the premise that he wasn't the masterful male before whom, so to speak, all society trembled. Such a prejudice could be of use if she could determine the exact method of employing it.

"The dowry can help you find advancement in a career to which you are obviously well suited," she pointed out with an amiably conspiratorial smile.

Turbayne rushed into the conversational opening that had been knowingly offered. "But is such a dowry enough to justify the grievous irritation of going through life with such a one at my side?"

Lady Kimball irritably refrained from pointing out that an Army career would keep him away for long periods of time. Even a dolt like the one before her would have reached that conclusion by his own minuscule powers of reasoning. "I am sure that an addition could be made to the dowry that was originally mentioned." She didn't relish the prospect of communicating this possibility to Marcus, foreseeing a discussion in which decisions she had already settled would be freshly questioned by him. Realism, however, was forcing that alternative upon her in no uncertain terms.

"Two thousand pounds *in toto* would be a satisfactory

dowry," Turbayne purred, citing the figure upon which he had determined his price.

Lady Kimball would tell him someday that she had been prepared to pay up to twenty-five hundred pounds in this excellent cause. She barely avoided showing contempt for the officer, as he could hardly be considered a foeman worthy of her steel. (Portia, however, was, on the whole, an excellent antagonist. As for Lionel, who ran off rather than confront her over and again, the boy was a coward. She felt affection for her only male heir, but knew a coward when he fled from her horizon rather than continuing to cross it.)

"I will agree to your receiving a dowry of two thousand pounds."

"Will Sir Marcus agree to this in writing?"

"I need not trouble him with such a small matter, but I will give you a note and say that my husband has informed me of his wishes in the matter and you are proceeding from that knowledge. I can assure you, Lieutenant Turbayne, that Sir Marcus will not attempt to escape any honorable obligation."

She smiled, hoping that such a circuitous procedure would postpone, if only for a brief time, the inevitable discussion with her husband. She would carry the day, as ever, but disliked seeing Marcus give up with a shrug and the statement that she was probably correct.

"Of course not, Lady Kimball. I had no intention of questioning the honesty of—"

"Further it would not be to his interest or mine to see a niece of ours living in the penury that an Army life enforces on those without sufficient funds."

"Very well." Turbayne nodded decisively, accepting the undeniable truth behind those contentions. "I do find it a comfort to know that I will be a member of the family of the heroic Colonel Alisdair Kimball and consider it a happy augury for the future."

"No doubt," Lady Kimball said briskly, being without patience for the pomposities of lower-class males. She spoke directly to the matter in hand. "The arrangements must be effected quickly."

"I will see the darling girl"—a pause, promptly followed by louder and quicker speech—"tomorrow night, then. An invitation to dine will mark a seemly occasion for resuming our— ahem!—courtship."

Lady Kimball was beyond astonishment at his assumption that she would ask an officer to dine at her table. Nothing could have been farther from her plans in the best of circumstances, and those did not apply here.

It was obvious that Portia, once again confronted with the domineering officer, would respond with disdain similar to what she had previously shown him. From which it followed that the girl must be married to Turbayne in such a way that she herself could have no voice in the outcome.

It was in the matter of arranging this outcome that Lady Kimball was temporarily daunted.

"When I used the word 'quickly' a moment back," she said, gathering her mental forces and cogitating at a furious rate, "my choice of term was perhaps ambiguous."

"It is a word that none can misunderstand," the steely-eyed officer insisted, jaw thrust out even further than nature had intended. "I am not such a fool as perhaps you take me for."

There was no time to debate this matter vigorously, it being at best a side issue.

"I should have said, 'as soon as possible,'" she overrode him, a plan forming in outlines even as she narrowed her meaning.

"I will resume courting her on this very night, then, at your dining table," the officer said. "That should meet the difficulty."

"I am aware that I have still not been sufficiently explicit, Lieutenant Turbayne. I should have said 'immediately.' Quite so. Immediately will be soon enough."

The lieutenant seemed to have been put at a disadvantage by the voicing of this fresh-minted proverb. "Do you mean that you insist upon the nuptials taking place now? Before I leave this room?"

"Such great expedition is hardly possible, but I sincerely approve of the altered nature of your perceptions, Lieutenant Turbayne."

"What course of action are you suggesting, madam?"

She was issuing a fiat rather than making suggestions, as both were well aware. No purpose was to be achieved, however, in underlining what was palpable.

"I suggest the utilization of methods favored by the Army," she said. "Surprise and stealth added to force in gaining the desired objective."

"Your knowledge of Army tactics is impressive," Turbayne admitted, his normally thrust-out jaw receding slightly in surprise. "For a female, that is."

She made no reply, confident that the unexpected silence would cause him to ponder what she had actually said.

The assumption proved correct. Turbayne's eyes widened slightly. "Are you suggesting," he whispered, "an abduction?"

Lady Kimball nodded.

"So you want me to spirit your niece away?" Like other men who claimed to relish the glory of battle, he was deeply shocked by female maneuvering.

"I repose full trust in your discretion, Lieutenant," she said, taking the time to soothe him and thereby facilitate progress. "I feel certain that you will do no lasting physical harm to my niece."

"Your confidence is fully justified, madam," Turbayne said, recapturing his dignity at this acknowledgment of tender feelings that may have existed in the bosom of an untested warrior. "Yours and that of Sir Marcus."

With the skill of a patroness of Almack's avoiding the company of a long-time friend in pursuit of a voucher for some

Wednesday-night assembly, Lady Kimball's features betrayed no feeling at this indication of her husband's complicity in the planned deed.

"Nor do I anticipate any difficulty beyond the first minutes," she added mendaciously, being unsure of the girl's behavior in such a crisis. "Portia will undoubtedly make some *pro forma* objections at an elopement. But these will fade when she realizes that her lord and master knows his mind."

"Yes, quite so." He was weakening at this salute to the quality he cherished most in himself. Seeking a fresh objection to keep Lady Kimball anxiously placating him, Turbayne could only conceive of a minor one. "I confess that I don't look forward to being married by a blacksmith at the tollhouse in Gretna Green, with one foot in Scotland."

"Such a dire eventuality is not one that I foresee," Lady Kimball said more easily. This last complaint she recognized as also being *pro forma*. The task was done and he had been fully persuaded to adopt the course she envisaged. "Among my husband's acquaintances is the vicar of the church of Sittingbourne-in-the-Vale."

"In Kent?" Turbayne seemed dubious, perhaps trying to determine whether or not it was beneath his imposing dignity to be wed there.

"Kindly permit me to amplify this circumstance for your consideration, Lieutenant. My husband, by some method that a mere female couldn't be expected to understand, was responsible for his appointment. The favor thus done has not to date been returned."

"Will the vicar perform this ceremony?"

"Yes. I can give you a note to Mr. Honeyman, informing him that the banns have been posted in London to no objections, and there has been a sudden change in plans as to the time and *locus* for the event. In regard to the license, I will add that it is in London but has been mislaid. Mr. Honeyman,

I can assure you, will not question the statements of a close relative of someone to whom he owes so much."

Turbayne accepted the conclusion that the churchman would not be prepared for any untruth from this source. It seemed likely, too, that the girl would have been bent to an Army officer's will by the time she was led into the vicar's presence.

"After the ceremony there will be less difficulty in repairing the omission of the license than you might think."

Turbayne nodded, firmly convinced that Bulldom's officials could be corrupted. "I shall need some help from good friends of mine, but everything will be done tonight."

"Portia must be got out of here by five o'clock," Lady Kimball remarked, adverting to the time when Sir Marcus would be arriving to prepare for greeting Jeremy Newlake. "Do that in any way you deem efficient. The less I know of the unimportant details in advance, the better I can feign surprise."

Turbayne didn't catch her up short on that point by reminding her that she had indicated Sir Marcus was *au courant* with this development. He was busily determining how much he could advance himself in the Army with two thousand pounds.

Hearing no objection and regretting that she had spoken too much even if he hadn't discerned it, Lady Kimball resorted to the handbell and obtained foolscap sheets and envelopes. Swiftly she wrote the two missives that would be required. After blotting the bold strokes with sand, she placed each note in an envelope and wrote an identifying name on the outside of each, then handed them across to the waiting soldier. Turbayne examined each with some care.

"The butler will see you out," she said, once again reaching for the handbell, this time before a magniloquent speech of gratitude might tumble from the officer's opened lips.

CHAPTER 16

For the third day in succession, Dulcie had been driven out to the park and then to the hotel front. Her wait for a glimpse of Ivor Turbayne and the opportunity to speak with him and decide beyond question if her feelings were returned had so far proved unavailing on this day as well. The procedure had wearied her so much that she was unsure of being at her best and brightest if the blessed Ivor did indeed materialize.

The doubt changed to a certainty, because her prolonged inconveniences were enough to bring on a headache. Mild though it was, she knew it would prevent her from being effective in dealing with him. Convinced that she had been badly used by fate, Dulcie instructed the coachman to return to Jermyn Street.

The trip proved longer and more uncomfortable than she would have preferred, of course. Alighting from the vis-à-vis without help, she gathered up the skirts to a high that remained becomingly modest and sped to the entrance of her home.

The door was opened by Daltrey, who stepped aside respectfully. One glimpse of the long and narrow anteroom with shiny furniture on the gleaming floor was enough to show someone moving in her direction. She raised her eyes and then they became wider in astonishment.

Stepping as if on parade past the painting of a hunt scene against the north wall was Ivor Turbayne. As before, his firm good looks were thrilling, and this despite the provoking tiredness around both eyes as if he hadn't slept for some time.

Feeling certain that if she remained in his path this human juggernaut would brush her away, she moved to one side. His head didn't turn and possibly he had not made her out against the sun's brightness after spending some time in the drawing room. She made certain that her shoes were noisy against the polished floor.

Ten feet off, Ivor's head turned slightly. For the second time, he was looking at this lovely fair-haired girl who he presumed was the Kimballs' daughter. He couldn't help regretting that it was the other he'd be marrying when this one was so much stirred by his presence, so pliable, so much more to his taste.

Dulcie made every effort to speak pleasantly, but knew even as the words were forming that the shock of seeing him added to her own headache would cause the voice to sound like a ghostly cry.

Ivor took it for granted that she was stunned into speechlessness by the sight of him. Under different conditions he would have liked to reassure this one and say that he wasn't really the awesome personage he appeared. At times, indeed, he could have liked to add, he had been known to take his ease with the best of them and be distinctly approachable.

He knew, though, that it was impossible to spare time for such a conversation. It was necessary to make arrangements with promptness for his financially desirable nuptials to another. Granting this lovely one a smile that was perhaps wider than might have been expected from a man of such a military demeanor, Ivor resumed his stride and left the house.

Dulcie didn't call out till she saw that Daltrey was closing the door, and then her voice seemed a harsh croak.

The butler, concerned, looked around swiftly. "Are you well, Miss Dulcie?"

She was far too stunned to hear him. She had seen it confirmed by glinting eyes and slack-jawed smile that Ivor was deeply interested in her. Very true. But because of varied accidents and what she supposed was the disapproving proximity of Mamma under the same roof, he had still said no word ever to her; nor had she, for other reasons, spoken to him.

"I take it you are not seriously indisposed, then, Miss Dulcie," the butler said after one knowing look at her mobile features.

Once again, Dulcie didn't hear the respectful tones. Vexed and thrilled, she rushed past the ever-visible Humility to Portia's room, where she could offer an advisory about this latest development.

"I saw him again at last," she said as soon as the door was closed, lowering her voice and keeping one eye to the door in case Mamma made one of her less welcome appearances. "I saw him, I tell you!"

Portia, already prepared for the evening and Jeremy's impending visit to offer for her, was looking out the window in hopes that he would arrive earlier. Hearing that Dulcie labored under febrile excitement, she turned away and further delayed telling her own good news.

"Well, what did Ivor say to you?"

No other question could have damped Dulcie's fever. "Actually," she began.

"Nothing?"

"Nary a word, I'm afraid."

"Then, you must have said considerable to him."

"Unfortunately, I did not."

"You haven't spoken to him and he hasn't said a word to you." Portia was surprised by such extremes of discretion. "Are you both tongue-tied?"

"In my case, a headache kept me from giving rein to my feelings."

"And what about the representative of the Seventh Foot?" Portia prodded, annoyed for Dulcie at what she conceived to be Turbayne's thickheadedness. Fool though he was, could even a Turbayne be toplofty when the right girl for him appeared in his ken? "Doesn't he have feelings?"

"In the circumstances, Ivor was unable to express them."

From embarrassment at this failure, Dulcie was near the point of losing her own temper. Portia, though eternally convinced that nature had not endowed her with the least tact, decided to ask two more questions of a different stripe.

"Do you have plans to see him again?"

"Of course."

"When?"

"I don't know," Dulcie blurted out, struck by the difficulty. "I will have to return to my vigil and cannot do so now—I cannot do so when I am ill."

Before soothing words could leave Portia's lips, Dulcie turned and ran out. Portia wanted to follow and redress the harm that had been done to Dulcie's esteem by the pointed questions. She had proved unable to calm Dulcie, yet her cousin had shown great gentleness when Portia herself had been greatly distressed at what she'd had reason to think was Jeremy's betrayal.

Determined to follow Dulcie into her room and pacify her, she stopped at hearing Dulcie pull a chair to the door so as not to be disturbed in her own room.

Dulcie, finding it necessary to rest until she felt better, lay back in bed. She recalled having been too upset to tell Portia that the desired meeting with Ivor had taken place here, in Jermyn Street. Portia would have been wryly amused to know that Mamma still actively sought to match Ivor with the wrong girl. She would certainly offer this news to Portia as soon as she felt better.

Portia was disconcerted by a knock on the door.

"It's I," said a female voice, respectful not only of Portia's status but of grammatical usage as well. "Humility."

It was indeed the plain-looking middle-aged woman who always seemed at work on the premises. The maid was carrying a sealed envelope on a silver-finished salver.

"For you, Miss Portia," she explained. "A coachman came to the door and gave it to Mr. Daltrey for you."

Portia's answer didn't conceal the surprise she felt. "Is some answer wanted?"

"Bless you, Miss, no," the maid answered, pleased by the sight of transparent emotion on the face of a family connection.

"Thank you, then. Thank you very much," she said sincerely, despite her knowledge that custom called for her to be condescending or offhandedly casual in dealing with the lower orders.

She was rewarded by a smile, and not till Aunt Kimball's personal maid turned to leave did Portia close the door.

The letter inside was brief. Addressed to her by name, it asked her to descend immediately, to leave the house and turn right, where she would find a coach with a door open on the side of the curb. There she would learn something of great interest to her.

Considering the last phrase, Portia felt that Jeremy was being dryly amusing. (She had no reason to think that another man might be adopting that phrase from a letter to him as written by Lady Kimball.) Presumably Jeremy had decided in advance that he wanted to see her before entering the house and Sir Marcus's august presence. The note was unsigned, which Portia felt was another example of Jeremy's celebrated discretion.

She reached for a cloak and mounted it over the white muslin with the green sash which she had brought from Sussex and seemed wholly suitable in color as well as cut. No one was in the hallway, not even the hard-working Humility. Had she encountered Lady Kimball, there would have been a risk of causing her aunt some additional displeasure by leaving abruptly. In this matter, too, luck favored her. The hallway was bare of Lady Kimball. She couldn't help glancing at Dulcie's closed door and hoping that the best of fortune would one day also favor this delightful and good-hearted cousin.

Hurrying outside to join the man she loved, Portia turned to the right. The nearest coach, with an impassive driver seated unmovingly, was a dull brown hackney. This vehicle would be far too dreary and large for the likes of any London-town gentleman. Beyond it no coach was to be seen. Not till she was five feet from the hackney, having made sure it was the only carriage in sight, did the puzzled girl become aware that sun in her eyes had kept her from realizing that the hackney door was wide open.

In confusion, she drew back several paces and halted to decide whether or not to press on. The hesitation proved to be a grievous error. Out of the open doorway hurtled a man dressed in an Army officer's formal wear. With a flash of startled perception, Portia recognized Ivor Turbayne.

She was vouchsafed one chilling sight of the man's purposeful face and determined steps in her direction. Even before she felt the first stab of alarm, Portia was turning to run back.

Turbayne, himself somewhat startled by a female who would offer the least resistance to him, acted more forcefully than might have been the case otherwise. Portia felt one of his hard hands around her waist and the other on her mouth. Terrified and helpless, the girl was being forced away from her home. A flash of anger overcame the other feelings and she kicked out back of her. A shod foot smudged Turbayne's white pants, but he was able to shift to the right and out of the reach of her retaliation. Such resistance caused the rascal's mission to take longer, but she was drawn into the coach and heard its door slammed shut. Angry and frightened, she found herself alone in this small space with a ruffled and almost equally angry Ivor Turbayne.

Lady Kimball had observed the episode from her window, to which she had repaired upon being told by Humility that a note had surprisingly been delivered for Miss Portia. Lady Kimball had left long-standing orders that she was to be kept *au courant* of any unexpected occurrences in her domain on Jermyn Street.

Most unfortunately, her niece had pulled back once she drew near the carriage, suspicions somehow aroused. Turbayne, as a result, had been forced to use more soldierly tactics than he must have anticipated or desired. Lady Kimball felt quite certain that nothing but Portia's self-esteem had been damaged, and she would be treated well if she chose to accept a suitable destiny and not carry on like some noblewoman resisting a male who was socially beneath her.

Feeling well satisfied, Lady Kimball left her bedroom and proceeded down the stairs. Halfway to the bottom she was met by an agitated Humility hurtling herself at a furious pace from the other direction. The maid's plain features were gray in distress.

"Oh, your ladyship, something terrible 'as 'appened!" she started frantically. "I seen it with me own two eyes."

Displeased, Lady Kimball didn't doubt it. The maid's attention had probably been drawn by protracted sounds of struggle through an opened window. Humility was, after all, a practiced spy on her mistress' behalf. Lady Kimball found herself taken aback by this efficient cerberus who had been thoroughly trained to see and tell.

"I am on my way to discuss the evening's service of supper with Daltrey," she said, which was true. "That is more important than any tale-telling."

"But your l—"

A response that was closer to Lady Kimball's usual attitudes was required, as she clearly saw now. "We will discuss this matter when I request the information, and that will happen very soon."

"Yes, ma'am, but—"

"Further, you will not talk of it with anyone else till then," she said magisterially, convinced that the maid's long experience would cause her to ascribe such a qualification to the mistress' desire to be the first one apprised of new happenings. To stamp that order into the maid's deepest sensibilities, she added, "Otherwise you will be summarily dismissed."

And she swept off, leaving an overwrought Humility behind her.

CHAPTER 17

Portia was hurled onto a seat as Turbayne shut the carriage door on them. The hackney, driven by a fellow conspirator in this abduction, started off. Turbayne was not in reach of her at the moment, but she was at his mercy. Beyond a doubt his feathers had been ruffled because of her resistance, showing a level of conceit to which men aspired but rarely reached.

"Damme, but you're a foolish vixen," he snapped, brushing at that pants leg which had been dirtied in the fray. "A certain amount of kittenishness is fine from a gel, but this sort of behavior goes too far."

Portia wanted nothing more than to do some further damage to him as the streets flew by and she was being taken by force from the meeting with Jeremy. But she had unwillingly realized the importance of subduing the extent of her feelings in any transaction with this irritable fool.

"I demand to be released," she said, keeping her voice level.

"Your demand is noted," he smiled, "my dear."

She did not know the diplomatic locution and assumed that his added familiarity was caused by elephantine teasing. Logic would be required on this occasion, posing a difficulty which was fresh to her experience. The uses of reason could not be denied as a last resort.

"I will have no hesitation in shouting, which must call the coachman's attention to this heinous act."

"A useless measure." The carriage made a right turn. "This coachman and the two footmen (did you observe them as well?) are dressed up to help me as a friend and fellow officer, my dear. We are all in the Seventh Foot, so your cries will be unheeded."

She would have been wrong to assume for even a moment that he was going to endure the presence of law-abiding males. That riposte surged to her lips, but was forced down. None of her mental resources would be spent at besting him in debate.

She suddenly looked out at the horses, wondering how soon they would have to be changed and thinking that she would make herself listened to on that particular occasion.

Turbayne had caught the glance. "No change of horses should be necessary before we reach our destination," he said.

Portia bit her lower lip in vexation, confirming his guess at what had been on her mind.

He added angrily, "You will regret any further attempt whatever to rouse my bad feelings."

The threat convinced Portia that she would have to do something which went completely against her impulses. She would have to wait, to be patient, to be far more devious than heretofore. But was that possible for her? She knew it wasn't.

As for Turbayne, he had not meant to seem like a cad. He only hoped to indicate to the girl that nothing untoward would be happening, that he was strong-minded but far from wicked, that his intentions were supremely honorable. The girl's continued antagonism was making it impossible to prove himself a true *chevalier*, and he determined on keeping quiet about the forthcoming marriage until his judgment indicated that she was better able to accept the truth of this circumstance.

And so the coach, with its cargo of passengers whose minds were in a turmoil, proceeded on the way out of Greater London.

Sir Marcus Kimball returned to his home from a difficult afternoon's gambling at White's. He had gone down quite a few more pounds than desirable for him at the game of macao, and didn't look forward to telling Beatrice of this setback. Prudently he changed for the evening and made for his library to await Jeremy Newlake's arrival. He ignored the bookshelves filled with the best available literature, settling back with an unread copy of Leigh Hunt's newspaper and the gossip therein.

Some moments later, in response to a series of dispirited knocks so low they could hardly be heard, Daltrey approached the door. Upon opening it to see who was outside, his usual deference gave way briefly to the glad cry escaping from his lips.

Lionel Kimball, glum-looking as ever, stood in the door, his face falling, his body slumped as much as possible for one who remained on his feet.

"Welcome home, Mr. Lionel," the butler said sincerely, having imagined the family scion as perished in some wilderness beside the ghost of the late Colonel Alisdair Kimball.

"Thank you," Lionel said, remembering his manners. Tentatively he walked inside.

Just as Daltrey was about to close the door, a man appeared on the threshold. This one had been standing next to Lionel all along, and the young man obviously knew of his presence.

The portly stranger was not of London, to judge by his clothes. As he was already stomping inside, Daltrey took three of his nimblest steps back.

"Who shall I say—ah, has called?" the butler asked frostily, far from pleased at any breach of formality.

"Stanley Galton," the newcomer boomed in a voice that would have shaken the rafters of Brooks's Club.

"Yes, sir." Daltrey was somewhat relieved. Miss Galton's other uncle had, at least, some connection in the house even if a time for his appearance here could have been chosen with greater cunning.

Before he was able to frame another question, Daltrey was aware that Lady Kimball had emerged from the drawing room, where her consultation with him about supper had been under way. Daltrey's greeting, so unusual in volume, had caused her to rush out and investigate the source of a butler's happiness.

The sight of her son brought a warm smile to her lips. Two sharp maternal looks convinced her that he was unharmed, but confirmation would be welcome.

"You are well?"

"Yes, Mother."

"And nothing untoward has happened? For instance, you have not been robbed by cutpurses or lured into committing marriage beneath you?"

Lionel looked too unhappy to rouse his faculties for a prolonged response. A preliminary shake of the head, however, was sufficient to convey his message.

Having ascertained that the goods had been returned in prime condition, her sharp eyes turned to meet those of Lionel's companion.

Many years had passed since she and Sir Marcus had ventured out to Sussex for a visit with her husband's late sister and her late husband—although, of course, both had been hale and hearty at that time. She remembered Stanley Galton from those weeks and particularly that he, like his niece, apparently had been born with little talent for dissimulation.

"Did my son come to you, Mr. Galton?" she asked, in lieu of a greeting.

Stanley nodded vigorously. He had removed his cap, but did not twist it in those large hands as might have been expected from an awkward countryman.

"I see." No doubt it was Portia who had advised Lionel to make his way out to Stanley Galton's farm in the ninth circle of England, and the knowledge offered another reason for contentment because of the certainty that Portia was safely out of harm's way.

"I brought him back," Stanley boomed, causing his auditors to wish he could have semaphored his meanings somehow, "not wanting to go against the will of the lad's parents."

She mustered a smile, convinced that Stanley Galton did indeed have a great respect for parental will, as he had brought his niece here a while ago and very much against the girl's wishes.

"I'm sure I can't begin to thank you enough for your kindness, Mr. Galton," she said, considering that the return of Lionel along with the disposition of Portia had filled her own cup of joy and all wishes of importance had been granted. The man deserved a well-bred dismissal.

Stanley, not moving, said, "I hope, ma'am, that I can talk to Sir Marcus now."

Lady Kimball saw no need for it, but assumed that a countryman who respected authority with Stanley Galton's fervor would be ill at ease until he had communicated with the man of the house. A swiftly spoken refusal might have caused him to wait in the house itself or outside, and common sense dictated the value of ridding the house of this nuisance. Her glance at Daltrey and his in turn were enough to show that the patriarch was at home. A tilt of her head sent the swift-moving Daltrey off to fetch him.

Sir Marcus emerged in moments, shook hands with his son and spoke some muffled words of reproof that ended in forgiveness. Only then did the dapper knight look up at Stanley Galton, recollecting that one of the man's brothers had been married to Sir Marcus's sister and another had been second-in-command to Colonel Alisdair Kimball (and no doubt, like the late hero, a fancier of the panoply that went with garish uniforms and all the perquisites).

In a voice that startled Sir Marcus by its volume, Stanley

repeated what he had already said about the boy's having appeared on his farm and the duty of returning him.

"Well, I'm much obliged to you, of course," Sir Marcus said, manfully resisting the temptation to squeeze both palms against his ears.

"Not at all, Sir Marcus." Stanley paused to frame further shouts. "He seems like a good lad, and he carries a heavy hatstand, if you take my meaning."

"It's good of you to praise his sense." Sir Marcus was at a loss about the words with which to finish this colloquy. "Again I do thank you for bringing him back."

"What he told me," Stanley roared in what he assumed was a normal speaking voice, "is that he's very interested in farming. Now as it happens I am always short of sensible persons to help with the headwork, with which farms abound, contrary to what you might think. And I am asking you for permission to let Lionel begin to learn from me how to handle things. I know that he would enjoy the work, starting as a land agent, and be useful and happy as well."

Sir Marcus sought in his mind for the terms to couch a polite refusal. Lady Kimball, confronted with this stimulus, remained unencumbered by such a need.

"That would be entirely out of the question," she said, speaking more loudly in spite of herself.

Stanley ducked his head in an approximation of courtesy to the distaff side but kept both eyes fixed on the patriarch.

"My wife is correct, Mr. Galton, for reasons involved with maintaining the entire family's position in good society."

Stanley turned only briefly to the imposing Lady Kimball, as if once more recalling her to memory. His look back at Sir Marcus showed pity, as the knight irritably observed.

In the hope of proving that he was indeed the master of his house and concluding this talk as well, Sir Marcus turned imperiously. But it was the butler to whom he employed his most commanding tones. "I feel certain that Mr. Galton would like to visit with his niece," he said. "Please see to it that Miss Galton is requested to descend."

Lady Kimball hid her feelings of vexation at what the next moments might bring and said very quickly, "I don't think that dear Portia is available at this time."

Uncertainty in a female gave the knight a chance to show greater firmness. "Daltrey, make sure of the state of affairs and report to us as soon as may be."

The butler glided out of their presence. They heard him in a brief, pointed argument with one of the maids, no doubt the ineffable Humility. She glided off to do his bidding, and Daltrey returned to answer another series of knocks at the door.

It was the expected visitor this time. Jeremy Newlake, having spent the day worrying over the outcome of negotiations to offer for Portia, had arrived earlier than expected to put the matter in train.

This early manifestation of the evening's guest was not the happiest of auguries to Lady Kimball, her nerves already unsettled by the happenings of the past minutes. Indeed she was beginning to feel that the overflowing cup of joy at her every wish being granted had just been suddenly and inexplicably drained to the bitter dregs. It was not a feeling that she relished, at all.

CHAPTER 18

Portia, in common with her aunt, was not experiencing a surfeit of happiness. She sat numbly in the hackney coach, well aware that she was unable to help herself by causing further difficulties. She would have to bide her time, hoping to employ a deviousness that was entirely opposed to her natural instincts. She sensed, though, that dishonesty was beyond her powers. As a result, she felt close to despair.

Ivor Turbayne, having subdued her, as he felt certain, congratulated himself silently for such decisiveness, not omitting a few additional thoughts of praise for the shrewdness of Lady Kimball.

"Now that you are better behaved," he said with a sincere smile, "I can give you the good news."

Portia ached to say that there couldn't be any of that variety. If she began speaking, though, she felt that her inevitable protests would cause him to do some physical harm.

"My intentions toward you," said the Pride of the Seventh Foot, "are honorable."

He was not a man entirely bereft of kindly instincts and had looked forward to seeing Portia Galton's face light up with pleasure at this knowledge he had just conveyed. It hurt him to see that the girl's expression didn't alter in the least.

"You do understand what I have said, my dear?"

No response.

Turbayne decided to make his meaning entirely clear.

"We are going to a church I know of," he added, not putting in that it was Lady Kimball who had apprised him of it, "and there I will quickly be able to marry you."

He could not have anticipated the girl's next reaction. Once it was certain that she found herself in no actual danger, Portia reverted to showing her anger unmistakably.

"This is an outrage!" she snapped, thinking at the same time that her current quandary must have been managed by Lady Kimball.

He drew back, prepared by this turn of events to revert if need be to physical action.

Portia decided quickly that if he was not acting on mere savage impulse, he might respond to as much logic as she could now find it in herself to muster.

"I can never make you happy or pretend to do so," she said. "I have promised myself to another."

Turbayne was infuriated to hear the best offer he could possibly make being declined by a female of no station. Nor was he best pleased by the looming possibility that he might lose the dowry which would purchase the career advancement he'd be able to use so well for his own benefit and the Army's.

"If you continue to give trouble rather than falling in with my plans, I will see to it that everyone knows about your having gone off with a male to whom you weren't wed. You must be well aware how much that will hurt you with any other prospect for marriage that you might think you have."

Portia's face colored in anger, and she had to restrain herself with the greatest of difficulty from clawing at this knave. She cared greatly for Jeremy and knew that he would understand and accept her explanation, but realized, too, that she would be putting him in the position of hearing sniggers of unbelief from others in society, that the scandal must gravely wound both of them as man and wife.

Turbayne, observing that she was in a condition of stunned silence, nodded his satisfaction. Once again he had shown superiority, convincing himself further that the tractable miss would make him an obedient wife, after all. Whatever her present doubts, she would later be pleased by his vaulting rise in the Army and her consequent elevation in social position.

While the carriage avoided Tunbridge Wells to enter the environs of Sevenoaks, the officer was experiencing a glow of great contentment.

Jeremy Newlake was introduced to Portia's other uncle, a countryman with a roaring voice suitable for berating cattle but somewhat out of place at a town house on Jermyn Street. He was delighted by Stanley's open manner, so much like Portia's, and shook hands warmly. Because of his stature as one of the most admired whips in *le monde*, his hand didn't suffer from the unwitting test of strength.

Stanley Galton, who remembered the young man from that occasion when he had brought Portia to London and had experienced difficulty with a coachman, took to him as well. The perfect combination of pinched-in jacket, white cravat in what seemed like a bed of collar points, and brown trousers strapped under shoes from Hoby's made for a superb turnout. On top of that, his grip would have done credit to a blacksmith. It was a combination with a neatness alone which the Sussex man found winning.

"I am glad you are here," Jeremy said, certain that the amiable countryman would help redress the balance in case of any difficulty posed by the Kimballs in giving their consent. "In brief, then, and scorning all manner of circumlocution—"

Jeremy paused at the daunting prospect of conflict in this one vital issue.

"Cut the cackle," Stanley said pleasantly, seeing that the young man was suddenly ill at ease.

Recalled to himself, Jeremy smiled at Stanley and then at

his friend Lionel, whose presence and return to London he had not previously acknowledged. "Scorning, as I say, all manner of circumlocution with a directness almost unknown from an experienced Member of the Lords, I—I wish to offer for your niece."

He extended his glance to take in Sir Marcus, who had unwillingly introduced peer and countryman, and Lady Kimball as well.

Sir Marcus winced. All of Bea's plans to marry off Portia to someone of no great position were being impeded. The girl had captured the heart of a peer, and Jemmy Newlake would have to be tactfully discouraged from attaining the goal he had set himself.

Lady Kimball's views, because of her additional knowledge, differed markedly. It was a matter of brief time before her niece's absence would be reported to the others. As the chit would soon be wed to another if she wasn't already a bride, there could be no harm in agreement with what was being proposed.

"So our own little scapegrace has won you, Jeremy Newlake," said Lady Kimball, smiling as if sincerely pleased. "I don't hesitate to offer my approval and I feel sure that my husband will agree if she remains your choice."

"Yes, I—yes, of course," Sir Marcus said hastily, in order to keep the peace. He had rarely been more baffled by a *volte-face,* and felt that Bea should have been more forceful by indicating that if Jemmy decided otherwise he would be forgiven. Jeremy, who had expected long conversations in which he'd have to utilize every ounce of his diplomatic skills, found himself nodding gratefully.

Lady Kimball turned to the countryman. "I can assure you, Mr. Galton, as my husband can, that few finer men than Jeremy Newlake are to be found in London."

"*Young* men, that is," Sir Marcus put in swiftly. "Few finer young men." He remained perplexed, but offered no further emendation, nor did he ask for the clarifying statement that he craved to hear.

"Well, if Portia wants him and you both agree," Stanley decided promptly, "I'll not be the one who stands in the way. It looks to me as if Portia might've traveled farther and done worse, sudden though it is."

This idyll of mutual agreement was shattered by the arrival of Humility. The plain-faced maid moved with Daltrey-like swiftness and showed signs of agitation.

Stanley Galton put the question that was in each man's mind. "Is this girl ill?"

"No, sir."

Pointedly she looked at Lady Kimball, not willing to speak about the matter in hand before gaining her mistress' permission.

Lady Kimball said, "Tell us if Portia will soon be gracing our presence."

Despite the strong feelings under which she labored, Humility recognized that her mistress wanted to hear some information but not all that was available.

"No, ma'am, she won't."

Sir Marcus interposed. "But supper is soon to be served, and Jeremy is here."

Again Lady Kimball made a point of seeking earnestly after knowledge when at least one of the men seemed helpless, an image that flattered her sensibilities. More important, it showed that she, too, was unaware of what had transpired.

"Is our scapegr—is Miss Portia in her room?"

"No, ma'am."

"Can she be somewhere else in the house?"

Humility shook her head, not trusting those words that lurked behind her closed lips.

Stanley Galton looked astonished, but Jeremy Newlake showed surprise only by the slitting of his eyes. Sir Marcus, already sufficiently discomposed, seemed unable to accept a word he was hearing.

The confusion offered Lady Kimball an opportunity to keep the men from making harsh accusations when they heard other details.

"I myself am not entirely startled," she said. "It now becomes necessary to tell you all that Portia has been attracted to another. An officer in the armed force. I have begged her to follow the formalities and be circumspect, but it may be that, young as she is, Portia finds herself impressed by the cut and colors of a dashing uniform."

Sir Marcus, who was convinced that such a passion might run rampant in his family's most distant connections, nodded at some premise he could at last understand. No doubt Portia had pretended to ill feeling toward Turbayne in order to excite the lieutenant and disturb aunt and uncle for having considered the groom's identity an established fact. Young women had done stranger things, to his personal knowledge and that of friends.

Jeremy, knowing about Ivor Turbayne and the problems that had been caused by accident, was unconcerned. Stanley Galton's bluff features, however, showed worry.

"I know Portia well, ma'am," he said in response to Lady Kimball's labored remarks about the follies of youth. "She is not one to go chasing about and decline to obtain any permission from her elders."

"Some girls change in character when they come to the city."

Jeremy, looking from one disputant to the other, naturally allied himself with the countryman. "Portia indicated considerable fondness for me."

"I'm sure she must have felt that, too," Lady Kimball agreed generously. "She has been most impulsive, however, since arriving to join us."

Stanley was about to defend his niece when Jeremy whirled around. He had heard a deep breath issuing from the maid's works, and looked pointedly at the rattled domestic.

Lady Kimball realized that the circuitous discussion had impelled Humility to the point of informing the others how much she knew. There remained an opportunity for subtly conveying to the maid that the others must be told Portia's departure had been voluntary.

"Do you by any chance know where Miss Portia went to?"

"No, ma'am, but—no."

"And you saw Miss Portia leave of her own free will?"

The last five words had been accented, but in vain.

"Oh, ma'am, I saw all of it through a window," the maid responded, so vexed that the truth rushed out. "She's such a fine person and I saw her being taken against her will and it was dreadful!"

"Let us be wholly clear about this," Lady Kimball persisted, hoping that the damage might be reversed by precise questioning.

Stanley Galton committed the *faux pas* of interrupting. "Who did it, girl?" he asked, his face reddening.

The maid, confronted by this apparition, turned to her mistress for an intercession which Lady Kimball plainly desired to make.

Jeremy, who was familiar to her, wasted no time in exclamations of dismay or lament. "Tell us exactly what you saw," he said in a tone that would brook no disobedience, "and be quick about it."

CHAPTER 19

Portia remained silent as the hackney coach lumbered away from the town of Sevenoaks. The likelihood of making Jeremy's life far more difficult through the taint of scandal, even if marriage between them was ever possible, had saddened her greatly.

Ivor Turbayne, who had raised the issue to quiet her and succeeded by that pointed thrust, saw her distress. On a kind impulse, offering needed comfort, he drew slightly closer to her.

Revolted, Portia moved to the farthest corner of the carriage.

Turbayne soothed his feelings at this small defeat by telling himself that the creature, for all her belligerent ways, wasn't used to men.

As her mood showed no sign of change, he considered some other source of comfort.

"Would you like to halt for some refreshment? I can have hot tea brought out to us from a wayside inn, so that you won't need to stir yourself."

She had looked interested when he spoke, by inference, of some contact with others, but relapsed into her former state at the codicil that was offered.

Turbayne decided not to raise the specter of temptation and fell back on speech, a weapon that had proved effective with her only a while back.

"You'll see, my dear," he said encouragingly, "that you won't regret the transaction."

The girl made no response to this olive branch of peace. Aware that she remained far from convulsed with happiness upon being granted such a boon in the marriage mart, Turbayne desisted in his efforts. It was enough for the moment that she was docile, and he would firmly see to it that she remained in a similar condition (which was best for himself and her as well) throughout their long married life, which was to begin that night.

The current visitors to Sir Marcus's home were struck silent by Humility's narrative, and the maid was crying upon being sent below. Stanley Galton turned to Jeremy, asking him to be patient for a few minutes, and then respectfully asked to be closeted with Sir Marcus. Obtaining a surprised nod of agreement, Galton further expressed the hope that the peer would permit his wife to join them. Lady Kimball, who could not have been kept away from what promised to be a lively contest of wills, nodded at Sir Marcus and was then requested to join both men in the library.

Left to cool his heels with a silent Lionel, Jeremy was soon joined by Dulcie. After a brief colloquy with the saddest brother a girl could ever have, Dulcie learned that the man whom she was determined to marry had abducted her unwilling cousin. Dulcie's reaction was to avoid the sort of swoon in which another well-bred young lady might have indulged, and she set her jaw while muttering darkly.

An observer, noting the sadness, paleness, and irritability of these three, and adding the knowledge of heated exchanges proceeding in the library as well as the agitation belowstairs of Humility, might have concluded that everyday life in this pillar of respectability resembled a Drury Lane drama of royal sacrifice in ancient times. The observer, blessed with wisdom and tolerance, might well have been correct.

It has been remarked that Stanley Galton, like his niece, was not given to indirectness. At this juncture, convinced that his niece was in peril, he showed even less of that quality than usual. He placed himself in a corner of the room, where his normally resonant tones would be further magnified, and made his demand.

"I want to know what you've done with Portia."

Sir Marcus felt his back stiffen aggressively. "I can assure you, Galton, that I don't know what has happened to the girl any more than you do."

Lady Kimball interposed. "What makes you think that we have been apprised of information which has not been given to you?"

Galton spoke directly to the knight. "Lady Kimball made every effort to get the maid to say that Portia had left of her own free will, and that determined effort proves she certainly knew beforehand what the maid had actually seen. But Lady Kimball hadn't said a word about it, meaning that she possesses what the law would call guilty knowledge."

Sir Marcus refused to accept the man's reasoning.

Loyally he said, "My wife wouldn't connive at such actions as you suggest. I deeply resent your insinuations and have a good mind to call for assistance."

Stanley Galton moved until he was in front of the door, blocking any seemly exit. It was plain from his demeanor that he wouldn't stir further until the knowledge he sought had been conveyed.

Sir Marcus shrugged angrily, but common sense dictated that he do nothing more.

Lady Kimball did not actually use the words "Infirm of purpose! Give *me* the daggers!" but they could have been sensed on her unusually mobile features. She turned to the countryman.

"It doesn't follow that even if I knew in advance of Portia being taken somewhere against her will, I can now tell you where she is."

As the family head was disposed to say nothing, Galton jousted with Lady Kimball. "From the little I've seen of you, I would be willing to put down my last copper on a bet that if you know of some event you'll make sure that you are told everything important about it."

Lady Kimball gave no indication that the thrust from a stranger had hit home, saying wickedly, "You will spend valuable time inferring my guilt and I in turn will repeat my claim of innocence till you abandon these misguided efforts of yours."

Galton's lips pursed briefly in thought. "Very well, then, if you won't give me the information I'll smacking well trade for it from you."

"Even if I knew where the wretched girl is to be found, it isn't possible that you could offer anything to compel an admission of guilt from me. If, of course, I were guilty, which I'm not."

Sir Marcus, looking at his wife as though he had never seen her to this date, was appalled to observe her completely enjoying this contest of wits and wills. It dawned on him for the first time that perhaps he had never fully understood his Beatrice till this occasion.

"I have to explain this matter, but will do it in the shortest possible time," Stanley Galton said, dividing his glances between husband and wife. "My brother Hosmer, as you may recollect, was second-in-command to Alisdair Kimball when they were both killed by the barbarous settlers in America. My brother remained alive for a week afterwards, long enough to write a letter home. This was brought by ship with his effects after he died and not examined by anyone else. My third brother, who lived some years longer, was the only one beside myself who ever saw that letter, and it's been kept in a safe place since we received it, you may be sure."

"'Letter.'" Sir Marcus had perceived the possible significance of this revelation. "You are actually discussing the contents, whatever they might be, of that missive."

"I am, Sir Marcus. My brother wrote that Alisdair Kimball

wasn't killed while leading a charge against the enemy from a hopeless position, as has been generally understood."

Lady Kimball, who had been prepared to brazen out any minor obstacle that might appear, flinched and closed her eyes tightly.

"Alisdair Kimball, whose heroic exploit is known to every schoolboy, was actually killed in flight from the enemy," Stanley Galton went on. "He was not only running but, I might add, gibbering with fear at the time."

Lady Kimball said automatically, "The document has obviously been forged."

"That aged paper and almost-yellow ink isn't a forged letter," Stanley Galton responded, almost with tolerance. "One sight would plainly show that."

Sir Marcus drew a deep breath almost of relief, feeling some minor satisfaction that a long-tormenting mystery had been truly solved. He could never accept the image of a heroic Alisdair that must have been put about by Army men wanting to tell of some prodigious exploit in a doomed affray. Alisdair had relished his prerogatives of being an officer, but responded to life-and-death danger just as Sir Marcus now knew beyond question he had done.

"I take it," said Sir Marcus quickly, "that what you want in exchange for the letter is information as to Portia's whereabouts."

"That's so. If I recover her unharmed, I will then pass the paper over to your hands. If not, I plan to avenge her by making that letter a point of public knowledge. I'm sure this is something you folk wouldn't want discussed in the London society that you inhabit."

Lady Kimball's features had whitened to chalk at the mere prospect.

A brief silence spurred Stanley Galton to add unnecessarily, "The longer you delay, the more difficulties you cause yourself."

"I can assure you, Mr. Galton, that my wife and I don't have the least information about the matter. Would that we did!"

The countryman's eyes rested on him, assessing the knight's capacity for planned mischief, then moved to meet those of Lady Kimball.

"Your family's reputation, Lady Kimball, and the social future of your children may depend on what you say in the next moments."

Confronted with the plain statement of risks for herself and her heirs, Lady Kimball promptly came to her own defense.

"Do you think I'd ever have let any true harm envelop the girl?"

Her aggrieved tone was a clear indication that she had previously burdened herself with guilty knowledge of the event, as Galton had said. Sir Marcus restrained himself from making critical remarks. A matter of more pressing importance had to be resolved before he could embark on a discussion about the nature of connubial obligations.

"Tell us where you've had her taken," Sir Marcus now said with all the sternness he could muster, certain that his manner was a match for Jeremy Newlake's as it had been noted a while ago.

Lady Kimball was already speaking, well aware that she had no choice but to comply.

CHAPTER 20

The drawing-room door flew open on the sight of Stanley Galton proceeding at a trot. Behind him, unnoticed by the witnesses to this awesome sight, Sir Marcus stared angrily at his wife.

"I must get to Sittingbourne," the portly countryman said, halting for the moment.

"Are you proposing to run there?" Jeremy asked at first astonished sight of so much agitated suet. Only then did he put his wits to work. "In Kent, you mean? Is that where Portia is?"

"The Army officer has taken her to a small church where the two can be married without banns or a license."

Dulcie, who had been paying attention to an elder as rarely before, called out as if with pain.

"Against her will, of course," Stanley Galton put in promptly, as if the point had been questioned.

"Definitely against her will," Jeremy agreed, jumping to his feet.

"Do you have a carriage outside, Lord Newlake?"

"Yes, and I have myself," Jeremy said, leading the way to the outer door. "I am a sport rider and will get us to Sittingbourne as quickly as may be." Still hurrying, he glanced around. "Do you intend to join us?"

"Indeed yes," Dulcie said sharply, determined upon confronting the officer with her knowledge of what she well knew was his perfidy, even though they had yet to speak with one another.

Stanley Galton, ever concerned about the reactions of parents, said censoriously, "Sir Marcus may not approve." He felt a kinship to the man after seeing his new attitude to Lady Kimball, and it was stronger than dismay that Sir Marcus had let his wife run rampant over others for so long a time.

Dulcie shrugged at the prospect of disapproval from either parent, not prepared to cope with it on top of the major disaster which impended.

And so the three of them departed, leaving behind the elder Kimballs and Lionel, as ever, immersed in his own unhappiness.

Jeremy had arrived in a dark brown high-perch phaeton, and spoke briskly to the coachman and two footmen attending his vehicle. These lackeys separated themselves from it so as to permit less weight to strain the horses. Galton helped Dulcie into the carriage and climbed after her, drawing a deep breath almost as soon as the carriage was in motion.

To Galton's momentarily disordered mind, the speed at which it traveled offered proof that vehicles would someday be invented to move quick as lightning without ever touching the ground. He heard the breath nearly knocked out of himself and imperiled his poise by reaching out a hand to Dulcie's and thereby keeping the girl from a fall.

"Oof! That was nasty," he said as they struck a bump in the road and he held her hand once more. Knowing that he couldn't help Portia till they reached their destination, he focused his mind upon the present awkwardness. "I think the hind axles are shaky, which shouldn't be an amaze, Miss, the rate we're moving at."

Dulcie hardly listened, busily framing the scornful terms with which she would confront Ivor Turbayne. She hardly noticed the vehicle's stresses, nor was she aware of Galton's helpfulness.

The farmer strained to look out. Streets passed by in moments, and all the houses appeared to be shaking.

"We're in Wratham," he said, and then frowned. "Or perhaps it's Chatham."

This observation was unheard by Dulcie.

"We could have been in Wratham when I started speaking and in Chatham when I finished," the farmer added.

Dulcie, considering a choice of ladylike epithets suitable for Lieutenant Ivor Turbayne of the Seventh Foot, made no response.

"I think he has to go through Tunbridge Wells, but I'm not sure," Galton said, further beguiling himself with formal matters as a way of occupying his mind.

Again the coach rocked and he kept Dulcie seated.

"Maybe it needs more oil in the axles," he said a little grimly. "Used to be that you had axles as would take three years' worth of oil, but not any more."

Dulcie was quiet, not aware how much time passed before the farmer said, "This looks to me like Maidstone. From here it's only a hop northeast, if I'm not mistaken."

Dulcie caught a few of those words and asked, "Can't Jeremy drive any quicker?"

The farmer, breathless from the speed and wishing with all his heart that they had already arrived at their destination, fell silent at this. He leaned forward in his seat once more as the phaeton charged into Sittingbourne at long last.

"I have been told that girls are very skittish about the actual ceremony of marriage," Ivor Turbayne said in what he assumed were comforting tones. "But I'm sure that a well-brought-up girl like yourself wouldn't want to cause a spectacle and make difficulties for other people."

Portia said nothing to this.

"At any rate, I'll be close to you all the while for the sake of reassurance," Turbayne offered. "I wouldn't put you through a ceremony I'd be unwilling to go through myself," he added, somewhat confusedly. "One doesn't do that in the Army, or in life."

It was a distinction that might have been explored fruitfully, but not now. Portia was so upset that she could walk only with the greatest of hesitation. She wanted this agonizing day to be done and told herself that she cared not at all what happened through the balance of her years on earth.

He was at her side as they followed the path which led to the southern entrance of the little church of Sittingbourne-in-the-Vale. The edifice was agreeable to the eye, with its refreshing lack of ornamentation and much-used, clean premises. At another time, Portia would have relished this house of worship and examined the loving detail with which it had been constructed and furnished.

A small gray-haired man of perhaps fifty summers, his lips quirked in a smile, emerged from an alcove to meet them. His rosy face was set off by clerical garb, his thinning hair gray. He looked contented with his lot in life.

"May I be of service?"

"Mr. Honeyman?" Turbayne asked, offering the letter which Lady Kimball had prepared.

The vicar accepted it and read slowly, his lips pursed at intervals. "'Change of plans,' dear me! 'License mislaid'—ah, that is most unfortunate indeed, most unfortunate."

Portia thought that the vicar might refuse to participate in a ceremony when no proof of statements made could be offered. The thought was short-lived. A broad smile lighted the vicar's face upon having read the signature at the base of the missive.

"And how is Lady Beatrice?" he asked, looking up. "And Sir Marcus, of course. Fine people, very fine. I owe much in my career to them, particularly Sir Marcus, and cannot refuse a request from these auspices."

His cheerful smile was somewhat protracted at meeting Portia's clouded eyes.

"Don't be afraid, my dear. Marriage, as I shall soon point out formally, is an honorable state, and I can add that you must in time appreciate and relish its fine points."

She couldn't bring herself to speak.

The vicar, hoping that he had offered effective reassurance, was distracted by Turbayne's gesture of irritation, perhaps because he wasn't being sufficiently noticed.

"And you, sir, are the bridegroom?"

"That is correct."

"We will need—"

At this juncture two of Turbayne's fellow officers who had previously posed as footmen came into the church, followed by the one who had pretended to be a coachman. They were revealed as officers in the Seventh Foot, previous disguises having been removed, and now appeared in the guise of officers and gentlemen.

"Ah, witnesses are ready before they can be requested." Mr. Honeyman seemed pleased at this essay in humor. "And is there a maid or matron of honor?"

"Such a person is not necessary to accomplish the purpose," Turbayne said promptly, as if instructing a subordinate.

"Formally, no, but it offers consolation to the bride if another woman is at hand," Mr. Honeyman pointed out, pleased by the bridegroom's eagerness to enter the blessed state of matrimony. "And I can say that a second female listed on the paper which I shall have to offer you as an addendum to the missing license, makes it all far more fitting."

"In that case," Turbayne agreed reluctantly, "someone has to be provided for the purpose."

Mr. Honeyman was already dispatching one of the witnesses to the courtyard, where Mrs. Honeyman might be found and brought back.

That good woman appeared belatedly, a small graying lady and the perfect match in temperament for her husband. She had been apprehended in front of the south entrance to the church, having been busily inspecting some damage committed by the arriving coach. At another time, Portia would have been delighted that the conspirators had themselves caused some delay, but it hardly mattered now. Turbayne had clearly shown that she would never be able to marry the man she loved and who loved her, so that nothing else mattered, not another witness, a ceremony, a future.

"My dear, you must not repine," Mrs. Honeyman said, embracing Portia. "Marriage is the end of one part of life and the beginning of another. The secret of a contenting marriage, as Mr. Honeyman and I have found over thirty-one years, is to have great respect for one another. It isn't always easy, but nothing that is worth having can truly be called easy, and marriage is a great adventure."

Portia supposed that the woman must have made similar remarks to a large number of prospective brides, but they were meant kindly. She could not have mustered an answering smile to save her life, never having felt less like showing cheer.

Mr. Honeyman led them to the lady chapel, which he said was in the best possible repair. He was busily suggesting a ceremonious but brief approach for bride and groom to the altar when Turbayne interrupted.

"The whole racket has to be as brief as possible," he directed.

"Your ardor does you great credit," Mr. Honeyman said delightedly, visualizing the rush that must have resulted in changed plans and a license mislaid. "Very well—ah, Ivor. I ask the couple to approach the altar."

Mr. Honeyman produced a Book of Common Prayer and some spectacles from the same repository, and settled himself.

"Dearly beloved, we are gathered here together in the sight of heaven," he began. Catching Turbayne's disapproving stare at this long-winded preamble, he smiled tolerantly. The peroration had begun and gently but insistently continued, offering guidance to the couple and reassurance to the nervous bride-to-be. This latter function took more time than even he had intended, as not even his best efforts appeared to soothe the girl. Her groom was clearly showing impatience.

A kindly gleam lit Mr. Honeyman's eyes as he turned once again to Portia. "Repeat after me. 'I—ah, Portia . . .'"

She couldn't speak.

Turbayne transferred the glower to that person whose delay was now prolonging his gain of an excellent dowry and purchase of greater advancement in the service of his country.

"Repeat after me," Mr. Honeyman said once more, patiently. "'I, Portia . . .'"

The need for a response woke in her that feeling which she had thought was suppressed. She couldn't feign indifference any more than she could feign some other emotion she did not feel. True, she would never be wed to the man who had captured her heart, but she did not want to marry Ivor Turbayne, and no dire warnings he issued could change her feelings or cause her to lie for the purpose of a marginally convenient future. That trait, for better or worse, was no part of her, and its absence had to be acknowledged now.

"No!" she said and shook her head fiercely. "No, I will not go through with it."

CHAPTER 21

The arrival of Jeremy's phaeton at Sittingbourne made it necessary to seek out the church building immediately. Slower travel was in itself agony to Jeremy, and brought painful reminders that his hands ached and that the horses were lathered.

Dulcie, in the carriage, left it to her fellow passenger to peer out anxiously. She was putting the last touches to those proper expressions of loathing with which she would speak to Ivor Turbayne for the first time, and keenly anticipating the opportunity.

Stanley Galton saw the edifice first, and called out excitedly. As the carriage didn't seem to be halting, he shouted, then pounded his feet on the floor in exasperation.

He had, however, underestimated Jeremy's resources. No sooner had he begun testing the shiny doorknob, with every intention to jump out while the vehicle was in motion, than it slowed even further and came to a halt before the main entrance of the church of Sittingbourne-in-the-Vale.

To leave the carriage was a strain, as his middle-aged body had stiffened after the hours in one seat. Dulcie, throwing off the lap robe which propriety decreed even in the spring for a carriage ride, was blessed by youth and therefore experienced no such difficulties. Jeremy, sparing a compassionate backward look at the panting horses, led the way into the small church.

No one was in sight. Their entrance had agitated the air

within this structure, and a verger appeared as a result. He was a spare man with arthritic fingers.

"How may I serve you?" he asked in that high-pitched voice unique to some of the partially deaf.

Jeremy knew very well that normal methods of speech would be fruitless, but didn't throw up his hands in despair. Instead he turned to the countryman.

"I leave this negotiation to your capable throat," he said, meanwhile looking around anxiously to discern signs of other human life.

"Where is the vicar?" Stanley asked, convinced that he was speaking more loudly than usual.

"Mr. Honeyman is conducting a marriage ceremony at this time," the verger said promptly. "I have not been able to participate fully because of a plaguey deafness, but after listening to you, sir, I feel that my hearing is suddenly much improved."

"Where is this ritual taking place?"

"In the lady chapel, sir, which has fortunately escaped the ravages of time for at least a few days."

"Take us there."

"Surely you can wait for Mr. Honeyman in the vestry."

"We must see him as soon as—as he's free," the countryman roared, inspired to partial prevarication. "It's of the greatest importance."

"Very well," the verger agreed after a pause in which Stanley had joined the younger man in looking around the premises. Perhaps he had no wish to lose contact with a gentleman whose words were clear to him. "Please follow me."

The verger found himself with one grim man on each side and a lovely young blond girl only some six feet behind. The route took them through a dim hallway and over to a plain double door at the other end.

The verger began, "It's all against my better judgment, you folk waiting here, but if you'll all just be patient—"

He halted himself, turning to the door when he heard a hubbub of male voices rising on the side, clear even to him. Jeremy, not having wasted a moment, had already gently nudged him to one side. Now he turned the handle and was first to hurry into the lady chapel.

The sight that met the newcomers' eyes was extraordinary. Portia, in white, was being addressed quietly by an older woman who had both arms about her. Three officers stood ill at ease, while a third, Ivor Turbayne, looked on the point of demanding that Portia stop this nonsensical parley at once. No one would ever know whether he had fallen temporarily silent because of some onset of scruples.

Jeremy took two strides in Turbayne's direction. The officer was startled by this procedure after so many others that had unsettled him, and made no defense against Jeremy's fist, which traveled suddenly and directly to his thrust-out jaw and tumbled him down to the floor.

"This is an outrage," the vicar protested with all the vigor of which he was capable. And his eyes having briefly met those of his good wife, "I have never experienced greater difficulty in uniting two persons in wedlock."

Jeremy looked astonished in turn. "Are you saying that the marriage has not yet taken place?"

"It has not, sir."

"Good," said Jeremy, Lord Newlake, whose discretion and capacity for harmonizing opposite viewpoints had become a byword in the Lords. "Nothing else saves this lout from a severe thrashing."

At the sound of his voice, Portia freed herself from the older woman's arms and whirled around eagerly, hardly able to believe in this manifestation. She said nothing, however, too deeply moved for speech.

As for Jeremy, he was aware of the wisdom that dictated not speaking his mind or baring his heart at this time. He saw none but Portia, of course, and unwittingly experienced some added good fortune in that the officer colleagues of Turbayne were themselves abashed by the recent demonstration of Portia's. Now they detested any thought of the roles they had taken in dragooning a girl into an arrangement she would plainly have loathed. Rather than take up the cudgels for their fallen colleague, the officers turned away.

Stanley Galton, breathing more heavily than was his wont, took advantage of the surroundings to raise his eyes and offer a silent prayer of thanksgiving. This devout and heartfelt gesture, keenly observed by the vicar, did much to mitigate his abhorrence of the intrusion.

As for Dulcie, she saw that Portia was in no major distress, then glared briefly at Jeremy and lifted her skirts to run over to where Ivor Turbayne lay.

"Can you get up?" she asked him directly, the well-rehearsed barbs forgotten in her anxiety. Those words were the first that she spoke to the Pride of the Seventh Foot.

It would be idle to pretend that the next minutes did not consist of much talking at cross-purposes, expressions of dismay, and anger mixed with gratitude for the outcome, and a modicum of nervous laughter.

Dulcie, like the still-stunned Portia, did not participate in this prolonged bout of exposition. She satisfied herself that Turbayne's physical faculties remained unimpaired, and received his astonished but very real gratitude and an admiring glance as well. She didn't look away until the other officers silently joined him in leaving the scene of what was to be his wedding.

Jeremy, having established *rapport* with Portia by way of eye contact and furtive smiles, permitted the anxious Stanley Galton to escort her into the vestry while he performed the same service for Dulcie. Arrangements were begun for the necessary change of horses to equip Jeremy's phaeton for the return ride to London.

This proved a leisurely trip, but not in all respects a happy one.

Portia had fallen silent because of the consideration that marriage to the man she loved still seemed impossible. It wasn't enough that Jeremy apparently loved her in turn. He may have lost his celebrated poise on confronting Ivor Turbayne in Kent, but wouldn't risk the obloquy of London society by marrying a girl in whose life there had been a questionable episode. Its details would certainly be trumpeted about and exaggerated by a vengeful Turbayne wanting to recover some self-esteem. The rascal would surely destroy her future without having to marry her. Nonetheless, she would speak with Jeremy and learn directly from him the full extent of his feelings.

Dulcie was concerned in another way with thoughts of Turbayne. Certainly he was the handsomest man she had ever seen and a strong leader with some tender feelings. Dulcie, whose mother was as strong in nature as her father was normally peaceable, felt strongly the attraction of a domineering male. With her mother's marital tactics rising to the forefront of her mind only after her own wedding, Dulcie would indeed subdue Turbayne accordingly.

These speculations, absorbing as they might have been at another time, were at the least premature. She would certainly discuss the matter with her parents, but was not hopeful of achieving the desired resolution without difficulty.

Stanley Galton found himself uncomfortable in the presence of two silent and preoccupied females. Jeremy, unlike the countryman, was fortunate in driving despite the labor and weariness, as he was spared contact with the breathing waxwork figures behind him.

The carriage arrived at Jermyn Street after midnight. From his driver's perch, Jeremy watched Stanley Galton carefully overseeing his niece's entrance. He decided to give Portia the opportunity for much-needed rest without further stimulus, and therefore refrained from joining them. Portia would be secure, beyond the slightest doubt, and he could return for the night to his rooms on Bruton Street.

Realizing that Jeremy had not come inside with Dulcie and Uncle Stanley, Portia assumed that she knew the reason. Her own tiredness led her to conclude that he was indirectly saying that he no longer had any wish to be seen in the company of a girl who had taken even an involuntary part in the night's wicked escapade. It was a scandalous matter, and everyone who heard of it would feel that the truth hadn't come out.

She was, however, far too tired after this bad time to give sustained thought to anything but sleep. It was possible for her to manage a smile for Uncle Marcus, a stare for Lady Kimball, and a nod at Lionel, the latter being far too sunk in gloom about himself to notice any response of hers. Then she embraced Dulcie and walked up the stairs to her room.

CHAPTER 22

Dulcie's father ordered her to go to bed, then saw that she hesitated. Unaccustomed to this source of authority, she looked at her mother, whose usually firm features offered no encouragement. Slowly, then, Dulcie started up the stairs as though prepared to join her family again at the first invitation.

Sir Marcus and his wife adjourned to the lower drawing room, with its methodically spaced furniture, impersonal neatness, and privacy for the talks that must ensue shortly. Here they were met by Stanley Galton, who spoke to the point.

"The marriage was not performed, for which we can all be thankful," he said, sparing a sharp look for Lady Kimball. "Some form of annulment could have been obtained in time, I suppose, had the outcome been different. But Portia might've had to spend a night with that rascal, and the taint of scandalous behavior would have dogged her for life. And might have made it impossible, almost certainly, for Portia to have a match worthy of her."

Lady Kimball, for once, lowered her eyes at a confrontation. She had been thoroughly chastened, for the moment, by her husband's rebellion. No doubt time and craft would return to her that power of decision-making and manipulating of others which she so cherished, but for the near future it would be important for her to seem the submissive beldame.

"I hope that Portia can spend some little added time here

without being hectored or bullied," Stanley Galton said quietly, for him.

"You have my assurance on that point," Sir Marcus responded with the utmost sincerity. "I shall see to it personally."

"Her stay here is unlikely to be prolonged," Stanley said, recollecting the affection to Portia that he had plainly seen in Jeremy's eyes. "As for the letter from Colonel Alisdair Kimball's second-in-command about his lack of—yes, I *will* speak more circumspectly, if you insist, although it's beyond me to guess who could overhear me through such a stout door as this room boasts. The letter, then, about the extent of the late Colonel Kimball's bravery, that letter I will bring to you during the next week. You may then destroy it if you wish."

"I do wish, Mr. Galton. Fervently."

Stanley nodded and opened the door. The image that met his eyes and those of the Kimballs was of Lionel, chin doubled on chest in what for that young man could hardly be considered an excess of his customary gloom.

Lady Kimball sensed an opportunity to give a desired order. "Your father wishes you to go to sleep immediately," she said, lurking behind Sir Marcus's new authority, because she had seen him wince at the sight presented by their male offspring. "You are to be fresh for a rout at the Duke and Duchess of Kinsing's home tomorrow night."

"I am not interested in routs," Lionel asserted with absolute truth.

"You will take your place among the polished ultras of *ton*, those who will attend this function as they do so many others."

"I want a place in another society but am not permitted to take that," Lionel was moved to say, doubtless encouraged by the presence of Stanley Galton.

It was a discussion into which the countryman did not wish

to be drawn. He hoped that the lad might overcome all objections, but great respect for the decisions of parents was enough to keep him quiet.

Sir Marcus felt a justifiable irritation, as so often before, at the sight of this young man's eternal gloom. In his new (if transitory) role as dominant parent, he acted on that feeling for the first time.

"Anything is better than seeing so much sadness in my home," he snapped. "Practice a vocation if you must and if Mr. Galton will accept you as an acolyte. I am sure that nothing can make you happy, but your family deserves a chance at happiness away from your presence."

Lady Kimball bit her tongue, refusing to make any comment after the previous heated discussions on this night, and in the face of her husband's unprecedented self-assertion.

It was beyond the imagination of either parent to think of Lionel as contented, but he did seem to straighten, and it was almost as though the beginnings of a smile had appeared on his lips.

"I can succeed and I will," he promised. "And then I will marry the girl of my choice."

Lady Kimball could not resist saying, "A peasant's daughter, I have no doubt."

Lionel was stung. "Faye's father is an honorable man."

Lady Kimball, unaware till now that her son's affections were engaged, asked, "Is he a peasant, the father of this girl?"

"A banker."

"Heaven's above!" Lady Kimball's sudden drawn-out hiss caused a candle light to flicker despite being set in a glass container. "A working man! Counting money with his hands, I presume! The dregs of civilization and wholly unacceptable in good society!" She stared at her husband. "This is the fate that you choose for him."

"It is his life," Sir Marcus said, adamant at recollecting past grievances against Bea. Nor did the presence of Stanley Galton fail to encourage his assertion of masculine prerogatives. "He must live it as he wishes and make his choices, whatever they might be, as a man should."

Lady Kimball threw up her hands in a rare physical display of emotion. Sir Marcus, for once, was left entirely unmoved.

Lionel's voice conveyed a feeling akin to enthusiasm as he spoke to Galton. "I can pack a few things immediately and be prepared to leave with you for Hove."

Galton's features sagged at the prospect of another coach trip so quickly after the recent foray to the clerical haunts of Kent.

Sir Marcus, perceiving that response, offered a much-needed balm. "Stay overnight here, Galton, and rest yourself."

"Thank you, Sir Marcus," the countryman said gratefully. "I accept with pleasure."

Blandly ignoring his wife's dismay, Sir Marcus directed her to arrange matters immediately. Lady Beatrice stalked off without a word, seeking the vigilant Humility, to whom instructions now had to be given.

Lionel led the weary Galton up the stairs. Sir Marcus, nodding with satisfaction at the knowledge of a day's work well done, heard footsteps descending and looked out to see that Dulcie was facing him.

Lady Kimball, materializing from the dining room, where the quest for Humility had taken her, looked outraged. The intrusion of Dulcie on her existence at this time was the last straw plus one!

"Your father ordered you to go to bed," she snapped.

"I can't now, so please let me speak with you both." Dulcie had heard enough of the discussion from upstairs to know that her father had been asserting his primacy, and was convinced she could beguile Sir Marcus into the concession that would ensure her a chance at future happiness.

Looking from one female to the other, a bemused Sir Marcus noticed the resemblance in coloring and eyes, as ac-

cented by Lady Kimball's face being largely unlined. Even
Dulcie could be spirited, but Sir Marcus didn't think that, like
Beatrice, she would ever treat others as though they were
playing cards to be shuffled around for reasons they wouldn't
necessarily understand or accept.

Because his wife was on the point of issuing one more
decree, Sir Marcus, in his present mood, was inclined to favor
his daughter's application.

"Come inside, where we won't disturb the others," he said,
turning to the lower drawing room. Behind him, Beatrice ex-
pelled a breath in fury at one more defeat.

"Now, young woman," he said, seating himself while Dulcie
respectfully stood, "what is it that troubles you?"

Dulcie took a deep beath and spoke part of the truth. "I am
disturbed because Lionel can apparently have the sort of life
he wants, but I cannot."

Lady Kimball, prepared to inveigh against any wish of Dulcie's at this time, was too astonished for a negative ruling. "At
the very least, one can point out that you are a female," she
said irrefutably.

"I am a female who desires to be waited upon by a young
man of whom my parents might not approve."

"Yet another resident who is in love," Sir Marcus groaned,
considering Lionel and Portia and the affairs of the heart
which had caused so much difficulty. "This house is becoming
a marriage bureau. If Humility and Daltrey suddenly decide
upon next making a match, it will be of no surprise to me."

Lady Kimball, not sparing the luxury of philosophical considerations, spoke to the issue that had just been raised.

"Who is this young man?" she probed.

Dulcie braved the likely maternal wrath. "He is an officer in
the Army."

"You must not see a man without social rank," Lady Kimball snapped; then her head shot up. Provoked by curiosity

and only able to imagine the worst on this night, she asked, "Is it Ivor Turbayne?"

Dulcie nodded. She was about to speak glowingly of his good points when an exchange of glances between her parents quelled Lady Kimball's next critical words. For the first time in daughter's or husband's memory, Lady Kimball rolled her eyes in an access of mute fury.

Sir Marcus was not inclined, at first consideration, to favor that officer's becoming a relative through marriage. The man seemed so puffed up with his own importance that spending time in his company would tax even the knight's ample store of patience. Unlike his autocratic wife, however, Sir Marcus was determined to hear his daughter's plea and consider its possible merits. "Does Turbayne reciprocate your feelings?"

"I know he does, Papa."

"Has he said so?"

"An opportunity along those lines has not yet arisen."

Lady Kimball interjected acridly, "When he considers the expanded size of the dowry he would receive upon marrying directly into our family, I feel sure that his approval may be taken as granted."

Sir Marcus didn't flinch at the possibility of spending more of the needful than might have been his lot otherwise.

Lady Kimball, encouraged by her husband's failure to impose silence just now, turned to Dulcie. "The man is a brute! You know of the foul manner in which he behaved to Portia."

"I regret and deplore it, as I am sure he does," Dulcie answered, recalling his crushed-looking features when last she had seen them. "No such outburst will ever come from him again, as the love of a good and determined woman will soften his feelings toward all females, in time."

"Marry this man and you become an outcast in society!"

"When Ivor is sufficiently prominent in the Army, as his abilities will make certain, the two of us are going to be accepted gladly by all."

Sir Marcus nodded in Lady Kimball's direction, accepting the truth of his daughter's observation. An ambitious, humorless popinjay like Ivor Turbayne would perforce be vastly successful at a career in public service. It was also evident that, with the promise of being yoked to Dulcie, he was not going to speak against Portia, as she, too, would be a connection by marriage. That made for another point to bear firmly in mind.

At this point in Sir Marcus's ruminations, any vagrant thought could have tipped the balance and established his sentiments in the matter. It so happened that the concept of Ivor Turbayne being accepted in society, as just promulgated by his daughter, was the notion that occurred. To advance in his calling, Turbayne would surely accept a dowry and marry into the immediate family of an Army officer who had actually been an ignominious coward in battle. That secret knowledge would make Sir Marcus enjoy his pompous son-in-law's company by appealing to his own sense of humor. Optimistic as ever, the knight also felt certain that Dulcie would tame her young man.

"Very well," Sir Marcus said finally. "I will have a note sent around to his digs and he will be waiting upon you in hours."

"Thank you, Papa," Dulcie said, eyes cast down modestly. To preserve the canons of formality, she added, "And thank you, Mamma."

Lady Kimball proffered no response, feeling unsettled. To herself she acknowledged that her husband was making decisions as never before and not letting her guide him along the paths she felt were suitable in family matters. Her initial perception of his growing weakness in this area might have been incorrect and never again would she be able to lead him. Apparently she had been ill-advised, for the best possible motives, to force Portia Galton, in vain, into the socially brilliant future that might now be Dulcie's. At the very best, some equality would now prevail between herself and Marcus in matters of choice, and that would be a source of dismay to the strong-minded daughter of Lucretia Armadale.

"Well, my dear," Sir Marcus said to his wife with unmistakable firmness, "family matters have been attended to. I suggest that we discuss these problems no further, but retire for the little night's rest that remains."

It was a suggestion which Lady Kimball accepted.

CHAPTER 23

Portia had not seriously anticipated gaining a night's sleep after all the turmoil of the day's difficulties. Weariness, however, had its way with her. She was awakened by sunlight seeping through the looped pelmets of her curtained window.

Hardly had she groaned at recollection of having lost Jeremy Newlake for reasons beyond her control than there was a respectful knock at the door. It opened on the maid Humility, who was freshly at work after perhaps an hour's sleep. It almost seemed as if no one else actually labored for the Kimballs.

"Good morning, Miss Galton," said the amiable drudge, her voice radiating good cheer. "Lord Newlake is visiting downstairs."

Portia felt a pounding in her heart, but then supposed this news was only the sort of gossip in which domestics traded. Jeremy Newlake's movements could no longer be of importance to her. Had he wanted to risk marriage with an outsider whose life would soon be burdened with a whiff of scandal, he'd have come into the house last night with the others. His having refrained was a tactful foreshadowing of a change in attitude.

Nonetheless she felt it must be of use to face up to the entire truth, to have her worst fears confirmed.

"Please ask Lord Newlake if I may see him," she requested.

"Bless you, Miss Portia, that's why he's here! He wants to talk with you just as soon as may be."

Portia felt a moment's hopefulness, but then told herself

decidedly that he would be informing her in a quick and discreet way that she must entertain no hopes from him any longer. Conveying such a message would require every last ounce of his diplomatic skills, but Portia had no doubt that he was fully capable of doing so.

She rejected Humility's offer to help with her wardrobe and addressed herself to the matter. A white bazeen day dress attracted her. It was high cut at the cleavage and with becoming pink and blue vertical lines to give her the illusion of greater height and complement her dark hair as well. This last she combed swiftly and arranged for the three curls to fall with an appearance of artlessness over the forehead and crowning all with a silver circlet she had brought with her from Hove.

One final look in the oversized mirror confirmed her opinion that she showed to advantage. Jeremy would at the very least be aware that a comely miss could have been his wife, and perhaps feel an occasional regret in later years that he had not availed himself of the opportunity.

She descended slowly, a hand on the staircase post. All seemed quiet. Sunlight through windows cast illumination, and she avoided it deftly as she moved, not wanting her features disfigured by even the trace of reddening.

The drawing-room door was wide open, and her heart pounded at sight of the keen-eyed, classic-featured young man who was the only one she could ever love. He wore a pinched-in coat jacket showing a white cravat tied faultlessly, and trousers strapped under the shoes. His white cambric shirt was decorated at the wrist with perfectly round coat buttons, making for a rig-out that was quite *le dernier cri*. He sat as stiffly as in a crowded brougham.

Now he stood, and she thought she saw a glint of admiration as their eyes met. Her face must have been as flushed as any trace of sun might make it, and this, she felt, was characteristically revealing in spite of her wanting not to show emo-

tions to that man who was about to dismiss her from his future life.

"Good morning," he said. "I trust you slept well."

"Thank you, yes."

"Very well, I hope." It almost seemed as if he were at a loss for words.

"Extremely so. From the moment I closed my eyes."

She had not intended to participate in any discussion of her sleeping habits. It crossed her mind that taking a seat might put him at some hoped-for disadvantage, impressing upon him that he was a visitor dealing with a young lady. Portia scorned this tactic as she had scorned so many others.

It was her own hesitation that seemed appalling. Instead of asking him point-blank if last night's alarums had altered his marriage plans, which she very much suspected was true, she was letting him dictate the course that the confrontation would take.

He smiled. It looked like a sincere expression of good will, but she didn't doubt that it was one of his diplomatic arts to make others feel liked and admired.

"I know that you were upset last night," he continued, "and I didn't go into the house as I wanted, so as to offer no distraction by my presence and thereby let you have the opportunity for as much rest as you needed."

It was devilishly plausible, of course. Was he saying that his plans toward her hadn't changed, or was he tactfully revealing that he felt his presence must no longer be important to her? His infernal discretion permitted him to offer information without enlightenment.

The direct question trembled on her lips but wasn't asked. She had not been aware of her own capacity for dissimulation any more than of Jeremy's for direct and uncomplicated action such as he had shown the night before. The knowledge was instructive, proving that persons could be contradictory under stress; but hardly helpful.

She decided upon prodding him indirectly, which she would not have felt herself capable of doing in the past. "And now that I've slept and am dressed, I plan to go about my business."

For a fearful moment she wondered if he would accept the slight sarcasm as a hint that she was excusing herself from his presence. Regretting the words, however, was useless. If he did indeed want her to remain, he would have to indicate his preference.

"You probably have no knowledge of last night's primary development," he said, stirring fresh curiosity without entirely resolving her dilemma. "Briefly, then, as I have myself just been informed, Ivor Turbayne will be waiting upon your cousin Dulcie with a view to marriage."

"That is splendid for her!" Portia spoke with the greatest sincerity, of course, being well aware how keenly Dulcie had wanted him from first sight of that handsome self-proclaimed autocrat. She was so pleased for another that it didn't cross her mind to ask how parental approval had been obtained. "I shall give Dulcie my heartiest good wishes."

He saw her sincerity and spoke to it. "I knew that your first consideration would be for Dulcie's happiness."

"Dulcie is a dear, dear girl," Portia said, surprised that he should make the point. "If she is determined to be happy with that man, then she will accomplish it."

"You are so pleased that you haven't yet realized it would no longer be to the officer's interest to soothe his vanity by telling others of last night's happenings."

It was perfectly true. Such being the case, she told herself joyously, Jeremy's desire for marriage to her couldn't possibly have changed.

"Not that it matters if he did say anything," Jeremy added now. "His words would not affect my actions in the slightest."

Once again she felt herself thrown into a turmoil, as his words carried two possible meanings. They inflamed an agony

she could tolerate no longer, and she opened her mouth to put the question to him irrevocably.

Jeremy, however, was speaking further. "When that officer becomes a distant family connection of mine, as seems most likely, I could not receive him at any of my homes."

Her first thought was that she and Dulcie must then continue to see each other and communicate by post. Her second thought permitted Portia to understand that he had, albeit indirectly, expressed his feelings.

"You are saying," she began, warm as if she were bathed in sun, "that . . . that . . ."

"That he will be a family connection of mine when we marry, yes." He paused, forcing himself in turn to ask a question that was difficult for him to put. "Do you agree with the course I feel I must follow in this dealing?"

"Yes," she said weakly, knowing at last what matter it was that he had exercised him for the past moments. "Jeremy, dear Jeremy, I am very happy." Her heart was so filled with happiness that it seemed impossible she could ever have doubted the strength of his feelings any more than her own.

"And I, dearest," he said, then reverted to another aspect of matters. He was unwilling to give himself wholly over to happiness until every difficulty had been cleared away. "As we had agreed, I spoke to your relatives yesterday about the plans we have made for marriage."

Portia's face was once more shadowed by anxiety. Surely every aspect of her future depended on these reactions! She could not conceivably marry without family approval, which seemed unobtainable, even for a skilled diplomat like Jeremy.

"You look concerned, my Portia," he said, taking her hands comfortingly. "Your uncle Galton, who happened to be present, commented, as I recall, on the suddenness of this choice."

"Doesn't he approve?" she asked in a small voice that she herself hardly recognized.

"Quite the contrary, my dear. He agreed promptly, if it's

what you want. Apparently he knows you well enough to place considerable trust in your good sense."

For that much, she was grateful. She had not even inquired what alchemy had brought this uncle to Sittingbourne, and suspected that it concerned in some way the gloomy Lionel, whom she had espied last night from the corner of an eye upon arriving back in Jermyn Street. There would be time for her to find out all the details of Lionel's adventures, but the time was not now.

A more powerful objection had occurred to her. The Kimballs could not possibly have given their consent, what with the maneuvers that had been performed by her aunt in attempting to cause Portia's marriage to the Pride of the Seventh Foot, maneuvers that had happily proved in vain because of Jeremy.

"It's hopeless," she said despairingly, then thrust up her head and narrowed both eyes in determination. "It can't be hopeless! I shall ask for permission repeatedly until she gives in."

"Portia, my dearest, you still don't understand." In the face of calamity, or so it seemed, he was able to remain sure of himself. "Lady Kimball did consent, last night."

"She . . . what?"

"Your aunt, not being as blessedly forthright as you, my dear, thought to impress upon me that she is a well-wisher of mine. There was no harm in giving the consent, as she saw it at that time, because she had reason to feel certain that you would very soon be married to Ivor Turbayne."

Such duplicity, as he had indicated, was entirely beyond Portia's capacities. She winced and shuddered.

"With that much done, your aunt cannot withdraw what was tendered before others."

Portia ventured to discuss it further. "I would think that she is now angry because you are a social lion, but her daughter's husband-to-be is not yet of that eminence."

"She is vexed, certainly," Jeremy nodded, having spoken with the Kimballs not long before.

"My aunt could somehow persuade my uncle to withdraw what was offered," Portia said earnestly. "She is capable of this action, using some mode I could never understand. He will follow her lead."

"Not any longer," Jeremy smiled. "Sir Marcus feels badly about what happened to you and has become far more inclined to assert himself as a result. I am certain, after seeing them very recently, that you will experience no difficulties from those two. Nor will you find it onerous to live with them until the happy day when you become my wife."

"Then, all is well," she said, still unbelieving the good fortune that was hers.

Now that perfect understanding had been reached, he spoke at last with the ardor he had previously forced himself to keep in check. "Portia, dearest Portia, I love you because you are the dearest and least devious person that was ever put on earth. Nothing that has happened between us has caused me to feel differently or ever will."

She came into his arms, and was received happily.

Stanley Galton, having spent the night, was prepared to leave for Sussex with the astonishingly cheerful Lionel. Before undertaking his third carriage ride in two days, he wanted to bid his niece farewell.

The impassive Daltrey directed him to the closed drawing-room door. Stanley knocked. There was no answer. He leaned forward and listened briefly, then smiled as at a memory and turned away. Daltrey was waiting respectfully for the conclusion of his prolonged visit.

Stanley Galton smiled. "It wouldn't surprise me to know that all is well with her," he said to the butler, and walked off.